CW00797615

Polar Heat

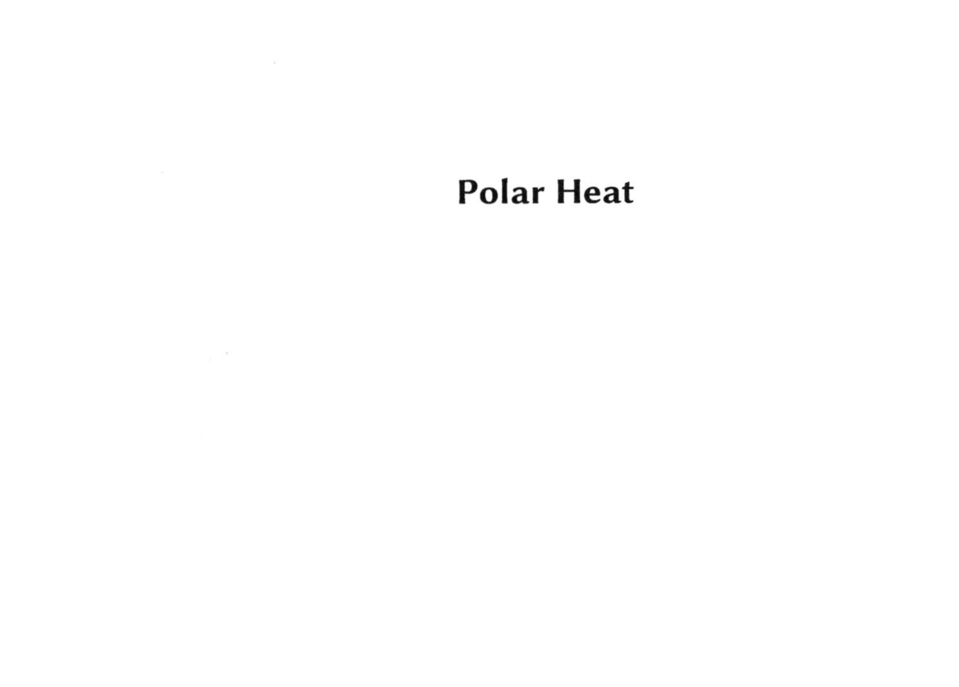

Polar Heat

Simone Beaudelaire

Published 2021 by Next Chapter
Cover art by Cover Mint
Back cover texture by David M. Schrader, used under license from Shutterstock.com
Large Print Edition

I would like to acknowledge my friends at The Wolf Pack for posting the picture that inspired this story, my beta readers: Sandra, Lisa, Edwin and Ch'kara, and my editor, Shay. I would also like to thank Next Chapter Publishing for taking the raw material of this story and transforming it into something readable.

This story is dedicated to Sandra Martinez, who helped me learn to see beyond what my eyes can perceive. Muchos gracias, lady.

Chapter 1

Russell "Russ" Tadzea stood on the tiny, makeshift runway beside his two-seater airplane and stared in disbelief at the woman before him. *Woman is the wrong word. She's a girl. A young girl. She can't be the teacher.* In his mind, Russ recalled the kindergarten teachers he'd seen on television. She'd be middle aged and plump, on the line between favorite aunt and kind, story-reading grandmother. She'd smell of cinnamon and peppermint paste. This… creature looked like a stiff breeze would blow her away. Hair the color of brown sugar swirled around her shoulders, tangling in the white faux fur lining the hood of her coat. Thin black gloves protected her fingers from the September cold. To Russ, it felt quite pleasant, with temperatures in the low 50s, so he knew she was not Alaskan. The girl met his eyes. Dark amber pools snared his attention, shining in the sun.

"Riley Jenkins?" he asked, and she flinched as she nodded. "You're the teacher?" he insisted.

She dipped her chin again, but not a single sound emerged.

"You need some sunglasses," he snapped. "Just because it's cold doesn't mean it's always dark. And I hope you have better gloves than that."

"Yes, sir," she replied. "I know a bit about cold. They're in my suitcase. It's not that bad right now." Her softly modulated voice, at least, sounded right. *Children will gather around her for Goldilocks and Rumpelstiltskin. I wish I could hear it.*

Shaking off foolish thoughts, Russ realized maybe he'd sounded a bit curt. Though the girl had responded without an overt show of emotion, her eyes had a suspicious glimmer and her lip seemed to want to tremble. *She'll have to toughen up if she wants to survive this remote wasteland.* But he still felt a twinge of guilt over his harshness. "Come on, girl," he rumbled, indicating the airplane.

She eyed it doubtfully and then turned toward him, one eyebrow cocked.

"Yeah, it's safe," he growled. "I've been a pilot since... since I was old enough to drive a car, and I know this little plane like the back of my hand. You'll be fine."

She sighed and trudged toward the tiny, winged vehicle. He opened the door for her and handed her up into the passenger seat. Closing it behind her, he scanned Golden, Alaska, the town that would be her home until... well, she didn't seem likely to last long here. Houses and cabins clustered around a grocery store, a café and a small church. Further back, out of sight, a few shops, a small movie theater, and various other local businesses interspersed among more homes. The K-12 school complex stood off to the right in a clearing in the dense evergreen forest. To the left, trees crowded shoulder to shoulder in a dense green wall. *Doesn't look like much to an outsider, I warrant,* he thought, even though the small city made him a bit edgy all by itself. He circled the plane and hopped into the driver's seat, quickly firing the engine.

"Have you flown in a small plane before?" he asked her.

"Yes," she replied. "One time my dad and I traveled in a plane so small it only had one flight attendant."

He opened his mouth and then closed it again, but a quick glance her direction revealed a smug look on her face.

"Tease me, will you?" he said with a rumbling laugh. "I may just have to hit a few air pockets along the way."

She giggled. "I hope you have good vomit cleaning tools... or a large barf bag. But seriously, no, I've never been in one this small. You sure it's safe? Wait, scratch that. Sorry. I didn't mean to doubt you." Her strange, whiskey colored eyes dropped to her lap, where her hands twisted nervously, mangling the fingers of her gloves.

Damn, she stopped smiling. For a moment there... he didn't dare put a voice to the entrancing image of Riley's smile. *Riley... such a modern name. It doesn't suit her at all. She should be called Grace or Elizabeth. Maybe Charlotte. Something with a lot of history and class.* "Don't worry, Miss

Jenkins," he assured her. "A lot of people, even people who don't mind bigger planes, don't feel secure in a two-seater. I don't take it personally. And I won't lie, you can feel a lot more than in a commercial jet, but that doesn't mean you're in danger."

"Okay," she said. "I believe you." She looked up at him and her eyes had regained their sparkle, though her lips remained still. No hint of a smile moved them. Usually when Russ growled at someone, he didn't think twice about the result. It was his nature after all, and besides, Alaskans were bred tough. It took more than a low-pitched voice to upset them. Riley, it appeared, was of a different sort altogether. Fragile, and by the look of her, quite sensitive. He wanted to be frustrated with that, to think of her going home – wherever that was – because she clearly didn't belong in Alaska, let alone in an area so remote that the kindergarten teacher had to work two days in one building and then be flown an hour away for her other two days. *But you don't really want to think that, do you, Tadzea?* He didn't, but he wasn't sure quite why. That is, until the scent of her washed over him, filling his senses with something undefinable. She smelled sweet and tangy and spicy, like every good thing in nature. *That's not perfume. It's just her.*

Russ sighed. Fragile, haunted-looking women were far from his norm, but Riley's scent touched a place in his heart he hadn't known existed. *I want her to stay.* There was no rational explanation for it, but the animal inside him trusted instinct more than reason. Instinct said Riley was special, and Russ accepted it without question. Only time would tell if his intuition had proven itself again, but since he'd be flying her from town to town twice a week, that time would be easy to find.

* * *

"Well, how did it go?" Russ asked as Riley emerged from the school building. She looked a bit shaken... *Well, a bit more shaken*, he amended silently. *She looked shaken right from the start.* She eyed him through the chain link fence that separated the playground of the Lakeville school building and the miniature airfield beside it. He indicated the open door of the plane.

Sighing, Riley tugged her bag up higher on her shoulder, zipped her jacket, and exited through the front gate, circling to him and scrambling into her seat.

"That well, eh?" he asked as he shut the passenger door.

Once he was situated in his own seat and had started up the miniature plane, she finally answered. "It was fine. How bad can half a day setting up a classroom be?"

"I'm sure I would be surprised," he said.

"Well," she admitted, "I'm pretty certain I saw the mom, dad, grandma and best friend's cousin's aunt of every kid in my class. I have eight on my roster and I think I burned myself with the hot glue gun more times than that because people kept popping in and startling me." She stared ruefully at the red spots marring her fingers.

The sight forced Russ to squash down an inappropriate urge to soothe her burns the old-fashioned way. "Well, it's a small town. Only eight kids in the entire kindergarten? No wonder they all wanted to be sure their little darlings are in good – though slightly scorched – hands.

Was anyone able to tell you what days you'll be needing me? They said you'd be here two days per week, but which days? And how does that work when you're teaching kindergarten?"

Riley sighed again. "How it seems to work is, I'll need you to bring me here Tuesday evenings and pick me up Thursday evenings. I'm working here Wednesdays and Thursdays, so I'll stay over those two nights. This is technically a half day kindergarten, only they meet two full days instead of four mornings or four afternoons. I'll be doing the same thing in Golden on Mondays and Tuesdays."

"Do you have a place to stay in Lakeville? I can't imagine there are rental properties there. Hell, there are barely houses. I suppose you found something in Golden, being as it's a bit bigger."

She tilted her head downward in a gesture of agreement. "I have an efficiency in Golden. It's kind of cute, and it has a day bed, so if I had anyone over, they wouldn't have to look at my worn-out sheets. But the kitchen is pretty good. It has an oven and four burners – well three that work, which is better than just a hot plate. They even threw in an old TV."

"That does sound pretty good," he said, knowing she was unlikely to have found better and could have done much worse. Not that the pay was bad, just that rental properties weren't much needed in a town with less than 10,000 people. "And Lakeville?" *What will you do in a town of only 750 people?* "Is someone letting you use a spare room or what?"

"Yeah," she admitted with a sigh, her eyes glued to the window. Below, the tops of spruce and pine trees seemed to reach for them, interspersed with sullen boulders with faces like trolls and the occasional sparkling lake. "The Carrolls have a son off in college in Anchorage, so they're letting me stay there when school is in session."

Russell made a face. "Did you meet Grandmother Carroll?"

One corner of her mouth quirked. "Yes."

"And?"

"She asked me if I was a werewolf, warned me to watch out for moose and bears and said I'd better not be a floozy."

Russ laughed. "Sounds about right. She accused me of being a werewolf once."

"Are you?"

Again with the unexpected jokes. When Riley let her guard down, her sense of humor sparkled like sunlight on clean water.

Russ affected a wounded expression. "Me? A wolf? God forbid. I'll never be anyone's dog."

His quip made her giggle, and the sound had just the entrancing quality he'd anticipated. She spoke again. "So what else do you do, Russell? Do you wait around all week for me to need hauling from one place to another?"

He chuckled. "It depends on the season. In the summer I fly tourists over the wilderness, or lead camping trips. I have some extra rooms in my house where overnight guests can stay. In the winter I take photos for nature magazines and travel web sites. I also manage the website for one of the local Native communities."

"A jack of all trades?" she asked.

"But a master of none," he replied, finishing the quote. It wasn't true, but it sounded good. And better yet it made her laugh. She shifted and that enticing Riley-scent took hold of him again.

I think I'm going to like flying this girl around... probably a bit too much.

* * *

A shard of silver moon slid to its zenith as Russ stepped naked from his cabin into the woods. The chill had not yet grown so great as to bite at him, though even when it did, he wouldn't stop his nightly ritual. It recharged and energized him. The light filtered through the trees and touched him, awakening his beast, urging him to shed the man and unleash the animal. Russ made no effort to resist. His body stretched and expanded, doubling and then tripling its size. His skin thickened and his muzzle stretched outward, his nose shrinking into a black circle on a white and furry face. He opened powerful, bone-cracking jaws and emitted a hoarse and rasping roar, setting the ends of the fragrant spruce and pine trees quivering. Rising onto hind legs, the massive polar bear extended its claws and scraped away at the bark of his favorite tree, one that already bore many scars from his efforts. Then he dropped back to the black pads of his paws and loped pigeon-toed, into the trees. The night was his to run, hunt and play in.

It took Russ a full two hours romping among the trees in the growing cold that no longer had any power over him before his body tired. As he sank into the snow, his animal mind filled with images of golden brown hair blowing in a gentle autumn breeze, of haunted, whiskey-colored eyes meeting his and then skating nervously away. His man wanted to protect her, to keep her safe from whatever past stalked her mind, but his bear's need was a little more pragmatic. It wanted to mate with her.

The thought of Riley drove his bear right up onto its hind legs and he roared with frustration, knowing a relationship with the young woman would be slow to develop. Then he hunkered down in a pile of pine needles and closed his eyes, drawing his consciousness deep within himself, to the place where man and animal existed together, in a constant battle for supremacy. Here, that tension generated energy to do what neither human nor bear could do alone. Here he could touch the minds of others. In his subconscious, he could see, clearly as he could with his eyes, the very spot on which he sat: a small hollow in the forest where the silver moon bathed him in icy light. In this place, he resembled his human self, though much bigger and bulkier, animal muscles stretching human skin. Reaching out with his consciousness, he performed an action he had not done in decades, one that could get him into a lot of trouble if anyone objected. The stars drew down from the black velvet blanket of the night sky and approached him, pinpricks of light like stationary fireflies. He extended his hand. "Will you come to me?" he asked in a low rumble. "Will you share your dreams with me, Riley Jenkins? The choice is yours."

A tiny orb drew away from its place and cautiously approached. He grinned. *Shy in sleep as she is in wakefulness.* "You can refuse," he informed the orb. "It's your choice. Will you share, Riley?"

The orb quivered and then zipped into his hand, where it rested lightly, warm and pulsing. The forest shifted and dissolved in a streak of green. Now Russ stood inside a small bungalow in a spare bedroom that had been furnished as a den and library. Darkly stained wood warmed the floor and bookshelves in a complimentary tone graced the cream plaster of the walls. Each shelf groaned under the weight of ancient leather-bound tomes whose titles Russ, in his mingled state, was no longer capable of reading, though the scent of the leather made the animal part of him want to nibble on the bindings. In a tufted burgundy armchair, a man with sparse steel-gray hair and horn-rimmed glasses sat with a child on his lap. The girl, who couldn't be more than about nine, wore a pink nightgown. Her light brown hair had been pulled into a ballerina's bun. Her whiskey colored eyes scanned the page of a book propped in front of her.

"The end," the man said.

"Daddy," the girl asked, shifting so she could look behind her. "Why did the girl cheat Rumpelstiltskin? He did what she wanted. Why didn't she just tell the prince the truth from the beginning?"

"If you think about it, dearest, you'll know the answer," he replied.

Her little brow furrowed in thought. "She was afraid the prince would be angry because of her father's lie. But why did her father lie about her?

He caused her so much trouble. He shouldn't have bragged. The way the story is written, it seems like lying and cheating are the ways to get what you want."

"You're wiser than your years, Riley. No, I don't suggest you learn life lessons from Rumpelstiltskin, or any other fairy tale, unless you consider whether what they seem to be teaching is right. Though maybe you should heed this warning: liars and tricksters are everywhere. Sometimes honest people get hurt by them. In this story, it's hard to see anyone as sympathetic. They all tried to trick each other, and the trickiest creature won."

"Is that how it is in real life?" Riley asked, and the wounded wariness already audible in her tone made Russell's heart twist.

"Sometimes," her father admitted. He looked down at his daughter's arm, his expression sad. A deep bruise circled the girl's wrist like a macabre bracelet. The way she shifted had a wincing, pained quality to it.

"Where's Danny?" she asked, as if changing the subject, though the expression on both their faces told Russ that nothing had really changed.

"He's gone, my dear one," her father said, and the girl relaxed, shoulders slumping. "He did... some bad things and now he has to spend some time paying for them."

"When will he come back?" the child asked with heartbreaking hesitancy.

"I don't know," her father replied. "He may be let out before too many years pass, but he will never be welcome in this home again." He paused, ink-stained fingers brushing lightly over his daughter's wrist. "I'm sorry, Riley."

Riley didn't speak. Instead she turned in her father's lap and threw her arms around his neck, shoulders shaking.

Stunned at being included in such a private memory, Russ withdrew... or he tried to. The dream seemed to hold him fast, to prevent him from withdrawing, something he'd never experienced before.

The scene shifted, pulling him with it. A streak of brown and maroon sped past him and suddenly Russ found himself standing in the strangest place. It looked like an ice cave, but one completely devoid of texture, each block perfectly smooth with only the faintest indication of seams. The room had enough height for him to stand, but his head brushed the ceiling. Uncomfortable at the tight, clutching space, he scanned for a door, but found none. He was trapped inside a white ice bubble. Russell's polar bear roared in frustration.

A soft answering sound drew his attention to his feet. Riley crouched on the frozen floor in front of him, her knees drawn up to her chest. Her face, in this dream world, had only half the attractiveness of reality. She looked plain, washed-out and tired, and the stink of fear obscured her enticing natural feminine scent.

"Why are we here?" he asked her. "What is this place?"

"You invited yourself in," she replied. "I don't know what this is. Maybe you can tell me."

"It looks like a prison," he said. "Feels like one too. Are you trapped here, Riley?"

She nodded. "I don't know how to get out. I spend most nights stuck between the past and this igloo, and I don't know how to break free. It's wearing me out, Russ; I never rest. But why are you here?"

"You drew me," he replied.

"No," she insisted. "You sought me out. I heard your voice calling me through the ice. You wanted to come."

"Yes," he agreed. "Because you drew me. From the moment I saw you, I knew."

"What did you know?" she asked. "What are you?"

He laughed, low and dry and without humor. "You are not ready for either answer."

She lowered her head. "After that roar, I'm sure that's true. I know you're not human. Maybe that's enough for now."

"I'm not," he agreed, "and yet I am. If you can accept so much already, it's certainly enough for now. We have time, Riley. Time together in my airplane. We can talk and find out if and when you're ready to know more. But I want you to know one thing. No matter what, when you're with me, you're safe."

"I'm never safe," she replied, her voice dark and sad, her eyes glued to the floor. "Never."

"Riley," he rumbled as the bear wrestled for control of him.

She lifted her face and those intoxicating eyes captured him. "I believe I'm safe from you, Russ.

That you wouldn't hurt me, at least. My heart tells me as much. But out there..." she waved her arm at the smooth walls of the igloo.

Russ reached out one paw, cursing at the sight of his nails, no longer the blunt, square human shape. Long, curved claws tipped each thick finger. Her eyes widened and she gulped. *Time, Tadzea. You must give the human time.*

Something tugged on his consciousness. Heat. Heat enough to melt the ice around them, and yet it remained solidly frozen.

"Morning comes," he informed the cowering girl. "I can feel the sunlight. If I come to you again, will you let me share your dreams?"

"I will," she replied. "This prison is so lonely. It would help to share it."

"Then I will come again, Riley."

She nodded.

The heat grew, drawing Russ out of Riley's igloo. He opened his eyes and was still a bear, lying in a clearing near his remote cabin. Even the chilly Alaskan morning felt hot under his thick white pelt. He lived too far south for his own comfort, except in winter. But he took the sun stoically, knowing the snow was on its way.

I wonder how Riley will react to the cold... I wonder if she'll remember the dream.

Russell had no answers, except that he would feel more comfortable without fur. Shifting back into his human form, he returned home, creeping through the trees in his yard to avoid being seen naked by his only neighbor, who was picking the last of the squashes from a luxurious vine. He barely managed to slip through the door and draw the curtains shut. Then, secure in his privacy, he stretched. Though much smaller as a man than a bear, at his full height, his extended hands brushed the ceiling beams of his cabin. He looked upward into the rafters, enjoying the sight of the raw arched wood above. His copper skin looked pale against the darkness, and thick muscle curved from every limb. *There's a lot me,* he thought, his eyes drawing down to the sculpted curves of his chest and abs, his bulging thighs. His sex, erect from sleep and from his dreamtime encounter with Riley, stood thick and strong from the silver curls at his groin. *I wonder what Riley would think of this.* Grinning Russ headed into the bathroom to take a shower.

* * *

The house seemed to have been carved into a low hillside, though the hill itself was man-made. Grass covered the earthen roof and a set of four rough-hewn pillars, set in close pairs on either side of the door, supported a tiny awning. Russell knocked once and then opened. A small room with a roaring fire invited him into pleasant warmth. A pair of leather armchairs supported a set of men. One, ancient and dressed in dyed-red caribou hide, toyed with a necklace of red and white bone shells. His copper-colored faced had been deeply grooved with age, and yet it retained a look of power and authority. He twined the beads in his gnarled fingers as he regarded Russell, and the nearly black pigment of his eyes had leaked into the white, leaving irregular brown spots.

"Father," Russell said in a quiet, respectful voice. "Randy."

He turned to greet his brother. Like him, Randy looked younger than he was. His sixty years rested lightly on his unlined face, though all three men had matching white hair.

"Son, welcome. It has been too long since you visited," his father intoned in his slow, careful voice.

Russell bowed his head, acknowledging the words. "A new school year is beginning. I was needed at many planning meetings. I came as soon as I could."

"Very good," his father replied. "You have always been dutiful, son. Please, won't you sit? I sense you wish to ask me something."

Russell sank to the brilliantly colored handwoven rug before the fire. "Yes, Father. I... how... I mean..." suddenly his words abandoned him.

Both of the other men crimped the corners of their mouths. Russell remembered the lessons of his youth. *Words are sacred. Do not waste them. Take the time to consider your words before they leave your lips.* Russell took a long moment to think. Silence was nothing to be feared among his father's people. At last he spoke. "I think I may have met my mate, but I'm not certain."

His brother's eyes widened. Though Randy came from the same parents as Russell, his life had been more human, and he'd had a wife long since. Children. Even grandchildren.

"Perhaps this is good," his father said. "I do not know. I see you seek answers, but I cannot give them. You are very much your mother's son. Perhaps you should contact your uncle."

Russell bowed his head. "There is wisdom in what you say, Father. I will do so."

"Will you be staying for the festival tonight?" Randy asked. "We are short a drummer."

Russell nodded. "I won't be needed back in Lakeville until Tuesday afternoon."

"Good," Randy replied.

Russell couldn't help but grin at the taciturn conversation. His life in town was so filled with words, he always felt the adjustment keenly when he returned to his father's people. *I wonder what Riley would think of this.*

Chapter 2

A week after his first meeting with Riley, Russ found himself waiting for her outside the Lakeville School building. He hadn't seen her in person since the other day when he had taken her to Lakeville, but after their first meeting he'd visited her dreams twice. She was willing enough to let him visit with her in her ice prison of sleep, but she had not shown him any more memories.

"Riley," he said, his voice gruff as he scanned her slender form. Something had changed about her posture. She was carrying herself with more poise, not hunched and nervous the way she'd been before. *Only two days in the classroom has done her that much good? Amazing. Some people were just born teachers.*

"Russell." She met his eyes and then her gaze skated away in what he had already figured out was a typical gesture for her. *Still shy, little Riley?*

"All aboard. How was your week? Ready to run for the hills yet?"

He shut her door and vaulted in beside her.

"I'm already in the hills," she informed him as the plane climbed to altitude. She pointed out the window at the small peaks – not quite mountains, but certainly big, rocky shapes, like mountains in miniature – that blocked roads from being made between the two towns and necessitated Russell's service.

"True." The girl seemed so serious, her attempts at humor never failed to surprise him.

And then she turned serious again. "No, Russ. I'm here to stay. At the very least, I've signed a one year contract. I won't skip out on that. And so far, the teaching has been fine. Of course, this is the honeymoon period. Kindergarteners can be little rascals at times."

"You sound like an experienced teacher. I thought this was your first assignment," Russ commented.

"No," Riley replied. "I've taught for two years already. Second grade, back home." She seemed to be fixated on the rocks and trees below them.

"And where is that?" he pressed, maneuvering the plane higher over a sharp boulder on the summit of the hill.

"Portland," she replied absently.

"Maine or Oregon?"

"Oregon." She still wasn't listening that closely. Worry seemed to radiate off her. *Not used to the plane yet, eh, sweetheart? You'll adjust.*

"No wonder you're sort of prepared for the weather."

"Pardon?" Now he had her attention. *Worried about the weather, I see.*

"I mean, Oregon isn't as cold as Alaska, but it's cold enough. So you're used to winter."

"Oh, right," Riley said, returning to her vigil, staring out the window.

"Hey, Riley?" Russell's heartbeat accelerated.

"Hmmm?"

"Has anyone given you a tour of Golden? You know, showed you the town?"

Riley looked at him out of the corner of her eye. "Kind of. The principal drove me around a bit."

"Boring Bill? Did it put you to sleep?" Russ laughed. She looked askance at him. "Sorry, I've known Bill Brewer a long time. I don't think of him as a principal. I think of him as the kid who put gum up his nose on a dare."

She giggled and then clapped her hands over her mouth. Her eyes were twinkling again.

"I won't tell him you laughed," Russ added. "Tell ya what. How would you like me to show you the town? We can grab a bite to eat at the café."

Her smiling eyes turned serious as she scanned him all over, lingering particularly at his head. He could hear her trying and failing to guess the years that separated them and wondering what everyone would think. "All right, Russ. Evenings are a bit lonely, what with me not knowing anyone yet, so I'd like to talk to someone for a while."

Russ grinned. *This isn't going to be so hard.*

* * *

Russell's prediction that getting to know Riley wouldn't be hard couldn't have been more wrong. The girl could give clams a lesson in being closed-mouthed. Apart from the fact that she grew up in Portland with a single father who was a clergyman and a scholar, the girl deflected every question. It was as though she'd been born knowing how to evade. Though he didn't like the secrecy, Russ had to admire her dogged determination not to let any details slip. Of her life in Alaska, she was an open book. Everything from the neighborhood she lived in to her phone number (he had that tucked inside his jacket – in case of weather emergencies) to every detail of her job had been thoroughly dissected. Russ had the distinct impression she was deliberately starting over. Trying to recreate herself without a past. He was inclined to let her. No need to pry, as long as she was willing to let him talk to her. He could take her on her terms.

Seated at the café with old-fashioned burgers, fries and root beer floats in front of them, he was able to face her straight on and admire the pretty face with the amber eyes.

"Somehow," she said, that funny half-grin twisting her lips, "you don't strike me as a root beer kind of guy."

"C'mon, Riley, everyone likes a root beer float. But what do you think? What should I be drinking?"

Her eyes narrowed and she scanned him again, and once again her eyes seemed to get stuck at his white hair. "I was going to say beer, American and on tap, but that's not really it. Maybe… scotch?" She shrugged. "I don't know a whole lot about drinks."

"Interesting choice. Actually, I wouldn't mind a beer on tap, though Belgian and Dutch beers are better. But I'm not overly picky. Around these parts, you take what you can get, and what you can get is usually booze so raw it makes your eyes water, even while it's warming your insides."

"Hmmm," she replied in a cryptic hum. "That's interesting. So you're a heavy drinker?"

"Who me?" He shrugged. "Nah, I was bred for this climate. I can take the cold. I only drink now and again. Would you be interested in joining me for a drink some time?"

Riley bit her lip. "I don't know, Russ. I…"

He reached across and patted her hand. "I know. You just got here. You don't know me well.

It's okay, Riley. I'll give you some time. I'll ask again later, when you're settled, okay?"

She heaved a sigh that looked like relief.

"Hey, I'll be right back." Russ stepped away from her and headed to the restroom. Inside, he took a moment to regard his reflection in the mirror, considering what a woman would see. Suntanned faced with crinkles in the corners of his eyes and grooves around his mouth. Thickly padded muscles in the shoulders and chest. Narrow waist. Sculpted, powerful thighs. And white hair. Fully white. Yes, in truth he was on the young side of middle age, but the color was congenital.

Should I tell her? Would that sound sissy, or like begging? He shrugged. The thought processes of women, and particularly of this woman he barely knew, were a mystery, and he couldn't guess what she would like or expect. *She'll have to take me as I am... or not.* Uncomfortable with his uncertainty, Russ abandoned the bathroom and slouched back the table, feeling grumpy. As he made his way past wooden tables with red vinyl booth cushions and white lights that looked like flying saucers, he noticed Barbara had approached with the water pitcher and was chatting conspiratorially with Riley. Russ drew nearer, unabashedly eavesdropping.

"So, how do you like our little town?" the waitress asked, smoothing her hair back into its ponytail.

"I like it," Riley said. "But I've only been here a week or so."

"Yeah," Barbara admitted. "It takes a while to find your place. I came when I was ten, but now I feel local. It's the people. They're reserved at first. Mind their own business. But once you plug in somewhere, you'll be fine."

"I'm not having much luck plugging," Riley admitted.

"It'll take time, but it'll happen. I hope you stay. We have the hardest time keeping kindergarten teachers. Mostly, I think, because they're young like you. There aren't so many single men here in town. Most of the young ones fly the coop after a year or two."

Riley's face flared scarlet, and Barbara hooted with laughter.

"Are you really so shy that the *thought* of dating makes you blush... or have you met someone already?"

Riley muttered something Russell couldn't hear, even with his animal senses.

"What was that?" Barbara asked.

"Nothing," Riley said quickly, almost snapping. "I've been here a week. I've just noticed... there are a few handsome men in town. I'm sure most are married, but... well... the pilot..."

"Russell? Oh, well." Barbara gave Riley a long look. "You know, I think I probably know everything about everyone in this town. If Russell is your choice, you could do a lot worse."

Riley blinked. "He seems nice is all, but won't people think it's odd, him being... older?" Her cheeks looked about to catch on fire.

If I play this right, I might just get with her after all.

"Not really," Barbara replied. "There aren't so many to choose from around here. Most folks are just glad if they can find someone decent. Russ is decent... and then some. I don't think anyone will give age differences a second thought."

"I'm not committing to anything," Riley said quickly. "I've known him a week. I was only curious."

Russ' bear roared in triumph. *If Barbara knows, everyone else will shortly. Riley will be considered my girlfriend by the end of the month.*

"Of course, of course," Barbara replied quickly. She refilled the water glasses as Russ slipped back into his seat.

Riley met his eyes and let out a startled squeak. She spent the rest of the meal in silence, staring at her burger as though she could eat it with her eyes. Russ let her silence rest. *Don't press. Just be near. Like gentling a wild beast. Eventually she'll realize she's safe.*

* * *

Russ' bear paws could feel the frost beneath the soil. All around him, plants withered, curling in on themselves to survive the coming cold. Under snow they'd wait for spring. Fall was most dangerous. The dying time. Without the protection of a thick white blanket, many plants failed to survive. Here, in the remote wilderness, no people ever came. No pipelines stretched across this lushly forested wasteland. Virgin timber stretched as far as his ursine eyes could see in all directions. Only scent and muscle memory told him he was on the right path. A pile of stones stood sentry. Russell raised his nose toward the pale sun, barely visible between evergreen boughs, and roared, announcing his presence. A bellow answered his call, and in moments two huge, white polar bears padded out from between the trees. Russell bowed his head in submission, refusing eye contact.

The larger of the two bears emitted a piglike snort and both turned and walked away. He followed. The forest grew denser, until the bears had to walk single file, squeezing between the closely packed trunks, until at last they entered a clearing before a large, natural cave. The bears rose on hind legs and the air shimmered around them. A man and woman stood nude before Russell, their hair white, but their skin surprisingly dark. Black eyes peered from beneath thick, white brows. Russell made no move to change. Not until the woman laid a hand on his furry head.

"Have you come in peace and trust?" she asked.

He dipped his muzzle toward the earth.

"Then rise and be man, Russell Tadzea," she intoned.

Russell stood and resumed his human shape. "Greetings," he said. "I have brought a gift."

"We know," the man said. "We thank you for the deer carcass. The scouts are bringing it for our evening meal. Will you stay and share meat with us?"

"I will, if you welcome me," he replied. Though the words were a ritual, Russell performed them with sincerity. They would smell exasperation on him.

"We welcome you," the woman replied. "Come into the cave."

Russell followed his escorts. Though he'd been raised here, once a bear left the community, he became as a stranger. Every visit provided a real threat to his life.

Inside, no fire illuminated the mineral-smelling darkness. They had no need of it. Several creatures, some appearing to be human, others in bear form, reclined on the pine needles that littered the floor. One tall man rose to his full height.

"Nephew," he bellowed, and his human voice sounded like the roar of his other form.

"Uncle." As he had before, Russell bowed his head in submission. The larger man clapped him on the bare shoulder.

"Why have you come?" he asked.

"I would ask you a question," Russell replied. "I think I may have met my mate."

His uncle roared with laughter. "You've become so human. If you think you have, you have. That's how it works. You scented her?"

Russell took a deep breath. "Her scent captivates me until I can think of nothing else."

"Then she is the one. Will you bring her?"

"Will you allow it?" Russell asked. "She's human."

His uncle blinked, face twisting in consternation. "Human? How can this be? Is she one of our kindred in the village?"

Russell shook his head. "She's not even Alaskan. She teaches at the school in Golden."

This, apparently, was more than his uncle could take in. The towering man sank to his haunches with an exhalation that was part sigh, part snort. "I have never heard of such a thing. And yet, your description of her scent, of your reaction to it, is unmistakable. But why would the Sky Bear bring you a human?"

"Perhaps she fears the bloodlines are growing too tightly connected," Russell suggested. "An infusion of outside blood could be beneficial."

Though werebears were not exactly geneticists, they recognized the dangers of inbreeding, which was why, ages ago, a blending with the local Native tribe had been permitted. Now both groups' numbers had again fallen dangerously low.

"There is sense in what you say," Russell's uncle told him. "And besides, there's nothing you can do about it. If she is your mate, she is your mate. Claim her."

"I will," Russell replied, *if she'll have me.*

Chapter 3

Two months passed. Nothing momentous marked the passage of time. Twice a week, Russ flew Riley from one location to another, and during that time they talked, slowly passing from acquaintances to friends. She remained reserved and shy, revealing little about her life or past, but the wait did not surprise or upset him. As nervous as Riley was, patience would be key. At night was a different story. Many times he approached her dreams and passed an uncomfortable night trapped in her ice prison with her. She didn't speak much at all, but he didn't mind. It was enough to be near her.

The Wednesday before Thanksgiving, Russ did something he'd never considered. He entered Riley's classroom. Inside, chaos reigned.

"Carl, don't even think about stepping outside without a coat on," Riley said sharply, and a little copper-skinned boy froze in his tracks, halfway through the open door. Noting the rebellious look on the tiny boy's face, Russ grasped his shoulder and turned him around, gently propelling him back toward his teacher, who was holding a green Ninja Turtle puffer coat.

Her eyes widened and she raised her gaze from kindergarten height, craning her neck to take in all six feet, six inches of Russell Tadzea.

"Why are you here?" she asked as she mechanically tucked the pouting child into his jacket and zipped the zipper. The kid rocketed toward the door where a hall monitor waited to escort him to the pick-up area.

"Bad storm coming in," he replied. "If you don't get back home now, you'll probably be snowed in for a week."

Riley grimaced. He knew her overnight accommodation in this, the more remote of her two buildings, consisted of nothing more than a spare bedroom in a family's basement. Fine for two nights a week, but not much fun in the long term. Especially since one member of the household was a cranky and half-deaf grandmother who shouted all night long. Riley always looked exhausted when he picked her up on Thursdays.

"I know," she said, grabbing another kid by the hand, a little girl with two long black braids this time, and stuffing her into a miniature navy blue pea coat. The girl pulled on a hat that had kitten ears before wandering into the hallway to wait.

"You'd better hurry," Russ urged. "We don't have much time. Remember, there's an hour flight between here and there."

"I know," she snapped, bundling up a third kid. "Damien, I've told you not to do that." On the other side of the room, a little blond kid froze, his hand against the yellow painted wall, where he appeared to be picking off a decoration in the shape of the letter B, covered in butterflies. "Come get your coat on."

The kid shuffled over to her and consented to be stuffed into his jacket.

Russ scanned the room. Four tiny tots remained, milling aimlessly as they awaited help with their outerwear. The room itself possessed a suffocating brightness, at least to his ursine sensibilities. Too much color. Too many patterns. Overwhelmed, he quickly looked back at Riley.

She had released the little vandal and moved on to the next kid. The wall picker looked to be headed the wrong direction. Russ placed a hand on the tiny back and urged him out the door.

She has to hurry. He grabbed up a thin pink hoodie with a unicorn on it. *Not nearly warm enough. It's below freezing outside.* "Who wears this?" he asked. A girl with her dark hair cut in a bob like Dora the Explorer approached slowly, clearly intimidated by his height. Taking no time to soothe the child, he shoved her into the jacket and shooed her out the door just as Riley finished her last charge.

"Come on," he urged.

She shook her head. "I have to be sure they get picked up safely."

"No," he growled, unable to suppress a hint of his exasperated roar. Her head shot up. "These kids are local. They have an hour to get across town. You have to leave now."

"They're babies. I have to be sure they're safe." Stubbornly she exited the room and walked the children outside.

Damned fool woman, Russ thought. *She doesn't even have her own jacket on.* He scooped up her tan coat by its faux fur hood and followed.

Outside, a cacophony of honking car horns – probably ten in total – and revving engines blended with the piping of adult and juvenile voices. Riley and the hall monitor, an elderly woman of obviously native descent, stood near the principal, directing kids to cars and bundled parents who had arrived on foot.

"Dr. Wolf," he said, drawing the principal's attention his direction.

"Yes, Mr. Tadzea?" she replied, raising one dark eyebrow at him.

"Miss Jenkins has to leave now. She has a long way to go. Doesn't her aid know all the kids?"

"Everyone knows all the kids," Dr. Wolf replied.

"So can she go then? I don't want to be caught out in the storm," he urged.

Dr. Wolf nodded. "Yes, of course. Miss Jenkins, get out of here while you can," she called. "We'll see you next Wednesday."

"Okay, thank you, Dr. Wolf," Riley concurred.

"Oh, Miss Jenkins," Russ added.

"Yes?" Her eyes met his. He held out her coat with a wry twist of his lips. She blushed and grabbed the garment before ducking back into the building. He rushed after her.

"Now what?" he called, his voice echoing on the cinderblock walls and tile floor.

"My purse," she replied.

Oh my Lord, women and their purses. Why can't they just shove a wallet in their pants? Rolling his eyes, Russell waited at the classroom door as Riley retrieved her purse from her desk drawer and dropped her ID and lanyard onto the desk.

No sooner did she turn in his direction than he wrapped an arm around her waist and dragged her out the door. The school building stood, not in the town, but about a quarter mile away, to allow for expansion. The miniature runway sat next to the school, separated by a chain link fence. *If I was a bear right now, I'd tear that shit down,* he thought, but he couldn't do that in front of all these kids, and despite sharing dreams with Riley, he wasn't sure she was ready for it either. Cursing with every step, he led her around the fence and all but stuffed her through the door into his airplane. Only then did he dare use his superhuman speed to round the vehicle to the pilot's side and hurl himself into the seat. A quick adjustment of instruments and they were off, zooming down the runway and into the sky.

Once he had pointed the nose toward their destination, he turned to Riley. She was staring at him with wide, startled eyes.

"You all right?" he asked gruffly before turning his attention back to the horizon. Ahead, the sky had turned the color of gunmetal.

"The storm was predicted to start at 2:30. That's why the kids were released from school at one. There should have been enough time. It's only 1:15, Russ. It will be tight, but we should make it."

He shook his head. "Forecast changed. Just got a message. Storm's coming sooner than they thought, but they're not making guesses. The wind is high and it's driving the clouds this way. Plus, it's barely freezing. No snow, not yet. That'll come later. This is going to be freezing rain. Lots of it."

Riley fell silent. Clearly she knew what that meant. He watched her out of his peripheral vision as her head turned slowly, scanning the sky ahead of them.

"Will we make it?" she asked at last.

"I doubt it," he said.

"I'm sorry." He turned and found her looking at her lap. *She does that so often.* He reached out and placed his hand on hers, where it rested on her lap. Her head shot up, turning those startled eyes to him. The burn of tears was every bit as intoxicating as the burn of the liquor they resembled. "It's going to be all right, Riley. You're safe with me, remember? This old bear has more tricks than you can imagine. We're going to be fine."

Riley appeared to be frozen. Her thigh under his hand felt stiff as plywood. But her fingers moved, turning her hand over and grasping him.

"Bear?" she asked, and the question had a pointed edge to it.

"In a manner of speaking," he replied.

She didn't answer. In silence they flew south toward her home base, toward the cozy apartment she was renting. How did she described it? A one room apartment with a nice kitchen and laundry in the basement. Much more her own home than sharing with the Carroll family. He'd never seen it, but Riley had a way with words, even over the drone of the plane's engine, and had brought the space to life for him. *I hope I can get her there tonight, but if not, my cabin is about halfway in between. We can land in the garden next door. Mrs. Tomei will kill me for flattening her squash plants, but the growing season is long done. I'll help her plant more next year.*

Russ put all his attention onto the airplane's controls, even though he didn't need to, just to keep his mind off the thick, undulating black clouds swirling on the horizon. The fact that they seemed to be racing his direction made him more than a little nervous.

Ahead, a high, rocky hill, not quite a mountain, loomed in the gathering darkness. *If I can get past that, I might be able to get her home,* he thought, urging the little plane to fly faster…*faster* into the storm. Then the sound he dreaded. First, the patter of rain on the exterior. Then the mushy splat as the drops began to freeze in the sky. At last, tiny pellets pinged all around them.

The plane grew heavy and sluggish as the freezing rain coated it, and the propellers did not like turning with a fat coating of ice. With the hill too far distant, he couldn't risk flying any farther. They would surely crash atop that peak and be left exposed, at too great a distance from any shelter. *What do I know about that hill? How can it help us?*

Before it, the trees thinned to an irregularly shaped meadow. *I can land. Worst case scenario, we stay in the plane until the freezing rain stops. Then we should be able to get to my cabin.* What he hadn't told Riley, and he wasn't sure she knew, was that following close on the heels of this ice storm, a blizzard was brewing and would be reaching them shortly. Their window to relocate away from the weather would be even shorter than the one he had raced to bring her out here, but at least he had a foolproof backup plan.

"Riley, I need to land here," he said. "There's too much ice on the plane. But try not to panic, we're landing, not crashing."

"All right, Russ," she agreed. "I trust you." She reached across and took his hand, squeezing gently. He squeezed back before laying her chilly limb back on her lap and seizing the controls.

With as much finesse as he could manage given the half-frozen propellers and rudder, he angled the plane toward the meadow. Riley's hands gripped together tightly and her lips were moving though no sound emerged. Russ had the distinct impression she was praying. The plane bucked and shuddered as they changed elevations, but he held steady on his speed and trajectory. *Almost there. I can make it.* Disaster struck before he was even aware it was coming. A thick, heavy branch from a tree just out of his peripheral vision smashed through the windshield at an angle, narrowly missing his arm as it embedded deep in the seat beside him. His grip slackened, creating a massive jolt and the resulting drop snapped the branch off from the tree, leaving it stranded like a stowaway in the cockpit.

Grimly, Russ hung on. The wind and rain whistled through the shattered glass, making his lips feel numb, not to mention his fingers, which were half frozen, gloves or no. It took every last ounce of his strength and concentration to level out their trajectory and steer the plane to the ground at a safe angle. A couple of graceless bounces brought them to a stop directly below the towering boulder-laden hill.

With a heavy sigh, Russ slumped in his seat. *That was too close.* His heart pounded and his bear threatened to rise up within him. He squashed down the beast. While the fur would be welcome in this cold, changing in the cock-pit would not be wise. *And you'd frighten Riley to death.* Riley. He had almost forgotten she sat beside him. Turning quickly, he assessed her. Un-injured, clearly, but she looked shocky and her lips were a disturbing blue.

Russ turned to their surroundings. With that broken windshield, the plane no longer provided any sort of shelter. But a dark depression in the rock in front of him stirred a half forgotten mem-ory.

"Stay here," he urged. "I'll be right back."

The ice slapped him on the back of the neck, finding its way inside the leather of his jacket to tease his skin with half-frozen droplets. Again he longed for his furry coat, but this was not the moment. As he had hoped, the depression formed a shallow cave. A few bats, but the only larger creature was in a deep recess, sluggish and nearly sleeping. Russ sent a message to the grizzly. *We're here as friends, brother. We will not bother your rest. Only let us shelter in the front of the cave an hour and we'll be on our way.*

The bear snorted a sleepy agreement. Satisfied, Russ returned to the plane, to Riley's side this time.

"Come on," he urged, knocking on the window. "You need to get out of the wind." She didn't move. Even her shivering seemed to have stopped. "Damn it, Riley, get out of there before you freeze!"

Nothing.

Yanking open the door, Russ lifted Riley into his arms. She hardly shifted position, as though she actually were frozen. *Got to hurry. No time to be timid.* Russ engaged his superhuman speed and raced along the slick and uneven ground, thankful it was rough, pebbly grass and not slippery pavement underneath. There was just enough traction to keep his sure, sneaker-clad feet steady. The rain fell harder, partially obscuring his vision, but his sharp animal senses would not be confused, and he entered the cave with a sigh.

Russ set Riley on the floor. She lay unmoving, curled up in the fetal position, her hands tucked into the opposite armpits. *She's too cold. I don't want to risk hypothermia. I have to warm her right away… but how?* Only one way presented itself. *Let's see how brave this girl really is.*

Quickly, Russ stripped away Riley's jacket and peeled the gloves from her clawed fingers. The thick leather and her quick thinking of tucking them in meant no signs of frostbite, though the skin was cold and red. Next he chucked her shoes into the corner. *She can't preserve body heat unless she has some to capture. I'll give her mine instead.*

"Riley, love, can you hear me? Listen, no matter what you see or hear, you're still safe. I would never hurt you. I'm going to get you warm."

Russ stepped back, remaining in Riley's line of sight and stripped off his clothes. He would need them later. Then he changed, flesh stretching and body elongating, until a wild bear stood before the prone young woman. She didn't react in the slightest, so Russ dropped to his haunches and cuddled up as close to her as he could get, nestling her deep into his pelt so his body heat could reach her. Then, with nothing better to do, Russ closed his eyes.

* * *

He'd entered the dreaming from the same spot so many times that to open his inner eyes and see the grizzly's cave startled him. He felt a bit disoriented, whether from it not being night or from the adrenaline, he wasn't sure. He felt like he'd been in a fight. Then, as he gazed at the dim and rocky walls, he remembered. *Ice storm. Plane. Riley… where is Riley?*

Inside the cave he could see no stars, no souls waiting to be joined in slumber. But he could see her physical form, lying on its side, curled into something large and white. *Me,* he grinned.

"Riley, are you here?"

The body before him began to glow and the glow coalesced into a spark, which rose and floated up in front of his face. He extended his hand, awed. Choosing to enter the dreaming from a wakeful state was a rare gift, and apart from himself, he'd only known a few Medicine Men who could do it. Riley's dream-self rested on his palm and the cave streaked away, leaving him inside their perpetual igloo, where she sat at his feet.

This time, Russ pressed his advantage, sinking to the floor and drawing her into his lap. She went without a struggle.

"Are you all right?" he asked, running his fingers up and down over her back.

"I am," she replied, more confident as always when she wasn't awake.

"Oh good, I was worried when you wouldn't answer," he told her.

"I think my lips were frozen," she replied with a dry chuckle. Then she glanced down. "Thank you for saving me."

"Of course," he said. "I told you you'd be safe with me. I promised you that."

"Instead, I put you in danger. I'm sorry, Russ."

"Hey," he said, rejecting her apology. He lifted her chin with one finger so he could look into her eyes. "It's okay, Riley. You know, the extra fifteen minutes you spent getting the kids ready would not have gotten us to Golden. That ice storm moved faster than anyone predicted. This was inevitable. The only question was where we would have put down. We should have stayed in Lakeville."

"Why didn't we?" she asked, not with pointed sarcasm, but as a wide-eyed genuine question.

"I guess I wasn't thinking straight either," he replied. "Now as I said, the storm moved faster than predicted. I thought we might have a shot of getting to Golden, or at least getting close. I'm not sure if you were aware, but behind this wintry mix there's a blizzard coming. I think both towns will be snowed in at least until the end of Thanksgiving break. I didn't figure you'd want to spend all that time with old Grandmother Carroll."

A ghost of a smile crossed her features. She smiled so rarely, as though the weight of whatever kept her subconscious in this frozen prison made a smile too heavy to bear. And yet, when he did manage to elicit a grin, it turned her already pretty face into something irresistible. *I won't be able to control myself around her much longer. I hope she's ready when the time comes.*

"So, Russ. Did I see what I thought I saw, or was I dreaming?" she asked, and his control took another battering as a spark of mischief flared in her eyes.

"I don't know," he prevaricated. "What do you think you saw?"

"I think," she replied, "that I saw my friend Russell Tadzea strip himself naked in front of me... and turn into a bear."

Russell took a deep breath. "You're not wrong. You weren't dreaming. Can you accept that?"

"Here I can," she replied. "I know I'm dreaming. I can pretend shape-shifters are just figments of a lonely girl's imagination."

"Do you really think it's necessary to pretend that?" he asked. "I've wanted for quite a while to tell you the truth. To let you see who I really am."

"Why?"

"You know why, Riley." His hand still lingered on her face, and so it was easy to lift her chin and lower his lips to hers.

Riley inhaled sharply though her nose. Though this was technically a sort of dream, she would be able to feel the sensation as though it were real.

He kept it light and undemanding, though his beast urged him to lay her on the far too perfect floor of the ice cave and claim her. *Can't press too hard. Can't scare her if I want her to be mine.* And he did want that. So to soothe her ever-present nerves, he ended the contact quickly. His bear roared in protest.

Riley's eyes had grown so huge, she almost resembled an owl. Her fingertips brushed her lips as though in disbelief. "Russ?"

"I want you, Riley," he said, his voice lowering to a growl against his will.

"You... you want.... me? How can that be? What do you mean, Russ? You want to do what with me?"

"Everything," he replied. The beast urged him to show her and he squashed it down, struggling to communicate coherently. "There's something between us, Riley. You have to know that. Tell me you feel it too."

He knew she did. He could smell her arousal, could feel the spike in heat every time he approached her. Her nostrils flared in his presence. Her eyes widened. In short, every sign of awareness in a human female manifested in Riley whenever he was around. He knew she desired him. What he didn't know, and needed to learn, was whether she realized it.

"I feel it," she admitted, breaking eye contact as he had expected. Then her head shot up. "Russ, are these dreams real?"

"They're dreams," he replied. "This place does not exist. It's a projection of your mind." Her shoulders sagged in obvious disappointment. *Ah, she doesn't like that it's not real.* He continued to explain. "But I'm really here, or at least my consciousness is."

She stiffened with a gasp. "So you remember these conversations? They're not just in my head?" she demanded.

"They're in your head, Riley. And yes, I do remember them."

Riley slipped from his lap and drew away from him, curling into a ball in the corner of her prison.

He approached slowly and laid a gentle hand on her shoulder.

Riley shook her head. "All this time I thought there was something wrong with me, the way I kept finding you here. How can you feel anything for me? You're handsome, mature, and confident. I'm nothing but a little mouse."

"You're not," Russ insisted. "You have a lot of fears, especially in the physical world. Believe me, I've noticed, but there's more to you than those fears. There is a smart, funny, fascinating woman underneath. A woman I want to know better. As... something more." Russ knew the words humans used to describe relationships. Girlfriend. Boyfriend. Couple. None of them made sense to him. He wanted her for his mate, but knew she was not ready for that.

When Riley regarded him over her shoulder, tears shimmered in the corners of her eyes. The sight set him burning so strongly that his bear's body grew aroused on the floor of the cave.

"Do you really mean that?"

He nodded.

"Russell, you swear to me this conversation is real, that you're really in it, and you'll remember it when you wake up?" She grasped his shoulder, and the fingers felt warm, no, hot. She was practically burning him with her delicate touch.

"Yes, Riley. I'll remember."

"Then tell me when we're awake. I want to know this is real."

He nodded. There was sense in what she said. *Remember she's human, Russ. She's been trained to doubt her feelings. I think this girl more than most.* "All right. We'll wait out the ice storm, and when it breaks, go to my house. It's not far from here. We can talk then."

Riley nodded. "Okay. So what do we do in the meanwhile, and will you know when it's time to move?"

"Of course," he replied. "My bear is quite sensitive to the weather. Would you rather wake up now?"

She shook her head. "I don't feel the cold here."

"You won't awake either. You're currently cuddled up in the coat of a polar bear. It doesn't get much warmer than that."

She turned to face him, and he saw that her lips had twisted into a strange expression.

"What's that look?" he asked.

"Do you have any idea how odd that sounds?" she shot back. "If anyone cuddled up with a polar bear, they'd probably end up as lunch."

He didn't bother to explain to her that bears didn't eat people, that they were merely territorial and aggressive. She knew, and was only making a quip. *At least she can joke about it.*

"Riley," he said, changing the subject, "I need to know something. Why are we here?" He indicated the cave around them, then caught her staring at his claws. *I wish these damned things didn't pop out every time I enter the dream.* Taking control, he willed them back into his fingers. "At first I thought it was a prison, that you were trapped in the ice, but that's not really it, is it?"

She slowly shook her head. "It's not to keep me in. It's to keep everything else out." She swallowed and her lip quivered.

"I didn't want to push you to share more than you were comfortable with, but this isn't healthy, Riley. What are you trying to keep out? What memories are you protecting yourself from? You seem... your reactions seem... like you've been abused. Did someone hurt you? A lover maybe?"

She laughed, a humorless chuckle. "No. No lover. My brother. He hurt me most every day of my childhood. And now he haunts me, even though he doesn't know where I am."

"I think I need to know about this brother of yours," Russ replied.

"Why?" she demanded. "I don't want to tell you about him. It's all in the past. I want to forget."

"Riley, love," he said gently, stroking her cheek with big, rough fingers, "if you can't even face your own dreams, it's still affecting you. If you want to start over, first you have to let the past go. That probably means talking about it, freeing the pain, rather than squashing it down inside."

"Are you a counselor or what?" she demanded. "What qualifies you to perform surgery on my soul?"

Surgery. Of course! The bear in Russ awakened and he allowed it to take control of only one arm. Long, thick claws sprang from fingers that were quickly spreading into a white paw with black, leathery pads. Russ took aim at the wall of the igloo and slashed. The fragile structure shattered, leaving them standing in the yard of the bungalow he'd once seen Riley in with her father. A tall, thin boy in his mid-teens held a much smaller girl, her arms tight behind her back. She struggled and wept, pleading in tiny, wordless whimpers as a bigger, burlier boy about the same age as the one who held her stepped forward.

"Danny, no," she sobbed. "Please."

The boy raked his fingers through a mop of black curls and set strange, ice-blue eyes on the child. Full lips twisted into an evil smirk. He laughed, low and menacingly, and then balled up a fist and drove it into the girl's stomach. Her breath expelled in a whoosh and she made a low, gasping sound as she tried unsuccessfully to draw in air. The boy laughed again, and this time the sound held a hint of manic wildness. Then he hit her again. And then again.

Russ stared in disbelief. "Riley, what?"

"My brother, Danny. Or rather, my half-brother. Father married his mother – our mother – when he was eight. I was born about a year later."

Russ gulped and turned away from the beating. Riley stood staring at him with haunted eyes. "Did this really happen?" he demanded.

She nodded.

"Why?"

She shrugged. "I was seven here. What did I know? I never knew why. I think he just... enjoyed it."

"What was he hoping to accomplish?"

"In this instance, to make me throw up. That was one of his favorite games. I stayed as far away from Danny as I could." Her expression and tone were bleak in a way Russ could never remember before, not from anyone.

Russell reached out his arms to Riley and she stepped close, allowing him to embrace her. She rested her head against his shoulder. Though she didn't cry, her body trembled.

"Is he the reason you came to Alaska?" Russ asked.

A movement in the vicinity of his shirt pocket suggested a yes. Then Riley lifted her head and showed Russ the most gut-clenching sight. Her big amber eyes had taken on a haunted, painfully sad expression. Without thought, Russ lowered his lips to hers again.

Outside the dreaming, at the edge of the cave, the quality of the daylight changed.

"Time to wake up, love. We have to get out of this cave before the blizzard hits."

Riley shuddered. "I'm not sure I'm ready to face the real world just yet, Russ."

"Ready or not, princess, here we go." He released the dream and opened his eyes. Lifting his ursine head, he watched as Riley stirred, stretched and rose to her feet, regarding him uncertainly.

"It's still me," he thought, projecting the sound of his voice into her head.

She jumped. "You can read minds?"

"No, of course not. That's unethical. I would never do that to you, but I can send you a thought. Forgive the intrusion, but this mouth is not made for forming human words." He sent a pointed look toward her pile of clothing on the floor. "Better get a move on. We don't have much time. I don't want you to get frozen again."

"Right." Riley quickly pulled on her shoes and outerwear. "Are you going to dress?"

"If I have to, but I have an idea that will get us to my home much faster," he thought. "Can you try to trust me?"

"I have no choice at this point," Riley replied. "What about your clothes?"

Russ looked longingly at his garments. "I can come back for them later. Though if you'd like to layer my coat and gloves over yours, it would probably be beneficial for you.

Riley considered the pile. "I have a better idea." She pulled on his coat, and then stuffed his pants, boxers, sweater and socks inside. She zipped his shoes into the pockets.

"Genius," he sent to her. "Now, time to be brave, sweet girl. Up on my back." He crouched down until his belly touched the floor.

"You're serious?"

"Come on, Riley. Let's get moving. We can sort it all out later."

Gingerly she slung a leg over his back and slipped her arms loosely around his neck. He could feel how tense she had become, but there was no time to soothe her worries. Already the patch of afternoon sun was beginning to darken, and he wanted to be in his snug cabin with a fire in the fireplace and something hot bubbling on the stove before the snow started. Rising carefully to his feet with his dainty burden clinging along his spine, he sent another thought, this one to the bear sleeping in the back of the cave. "Thank you, Brother. Be well."

He received only a snore in reply, and then he stepped out into the cold.

Riley inhaled sharply as the icy air hit her, but there was no time to adjust. Russell's instincts told him which way to go. East by southeast, away from the rock. What sun still shone through roiling gray clouds stood a bit behind them, indicating midafternoon. He began to walk, making sure Riley had a secure hold on him and wouldn't fall. Then, as he entered the tree line, he changed to a trot along trails made by deer, widened by the broad paws of his kindred over untold centuries.

The air hung still and cold, with an eerie sense of heaviness to it. His trot became a comfortable lope that ate up the distance easily. No need for superhuman speed, and he didn't want to strain Riley too greatly. That she had climbed onto his back instead of panicking spoke well of her resiliency. In fact, the more they ran, the more she seemed to relax. Her body molded to his and her hold on his neck didn't tighten to a strangling force. She simply allowed him to carry them away from the killing storm to a place of true safety.

The trees overhead had caught the brunt of the weather, with snapped tops and branches lying here and there, but the ground was mostly clear of ice. Not that it mattered. His paws were well adapted to moving across ice with speed and surety.

The trees surrounded them in a green and fragrant cocoon through which he wove easily without ever slowing his pace. His cabin called him like a beacon. The temperature dropped as he ran Riley through the uncharted forest, and he could feel her body stiffen and begin to tremble. Praying she would be able to hold on, he dared increase his speed slightly. *Only a quarter of a mile to go. We can make it. Easy, easy does it. Hold on, Riley, we're almost home.*

A fat white drop landed on his nose and stung as it melted. Other flakes drifted lazily past his face. *First snowfall of the year. It will take a while to become a problem.* An eighth of a mile left. A tenth. A few yards. He burst through the trees into the clearing he shared with Mrs. Tomei. A quick glance showed her nowhere in sight, but the lights glowed in her cabin windows and smoke drifted from her chimney. Russ used a burst of extra speed to hurry them out of the line of sight of her kitchen window and around the far side of his cabin, where he finally stopped in the snowy yard. Crouching, he allowed Riley to slide from his back. She rose to her feet, though not entirely steadily, and stared in awe at the snow.

He nudged her with his nose. "Watch from inside," he said into her mind. "You've gotten chilled enough for one day."

She nodded and followed him to the front door. From here, Mrs. Tomei might be able to see him, but it was unlikely.

"Open the door. The key is under the lower left brick, second from the bottom."

Riley examined the wall by the door and ran a finger along the shattered mortar. Then she slipped the brick from its place and reached inside. His oversized gloves hindered her quest and she caught one finger between her teeth, yanking it off and trying again. This time she was able to grasp her quarry and extract it from the crevice, fitting it into the lock with ease.

Opening the door, she quickly returned the key and then the brick before slipping through. Once she was inside, Russ spared another glance at Mrs. Tomei's house, but his ursine eyes were not quite strong enough to see if her frail form stood at the window. Shrugging, he drew his bear inward, into the center of his being and became a man again.

The cold stung his bare skin, and he hurried inside, shutting out the cold and the storm.

Chapter 4

Russell flipped on the light switch, thankful the power was still on… for the moment. Riley gasped.

"What?" he asked.

"You… you… you're naked," she burst out, turning her back on him as though examining the wall with great intensity.

"Oh, right. Sorry. I'll be right back." Grinning, he stalked through his great room and into the bedroom, where he pulled out a pair of lounge pants and a sweatshirt. *Might as well be comfortable.* When he returned to the living room, he found Riley still standing by the wall, looking nervous.

"Welcome to my home," he intoned, sweeping his arm to take in the space.

She turned to him, blinking. Then she looked around, apparently noting the sofa made of rough-hewn logs and cushions upholstered in red and black plaid, two leather armchairs, a brick fireplace, and a kitchen along one wall. A door led to his master suite. A staircase opened into a loft with guest bedrooms lining a balcony.

"Nice place," she said. "Um, do you have a bathroom I could use? The cold, you know."

"Sure," Russell replied. "You can use mine, in the master suite, or the guest bathroom. He indicated a door off the great room.

She opted for the second choice and dashed away. Clearly, she felt uncomfortable. *But with being in my home. I can't believe how easily she accepted everything else.* Feeling more positive than he could remember being in ages, Russ meandered to the window and glanced out. The swirling flakes that had chased them home had thickened into an almost impenetrable curtain of white.

Russ hunted down his spare cell phone and called the Golden School District office.

"Mr. Brewer," he said to the principal, who had answered the phone. "This is Russ Tadzea. I wanted to let you know that I have Miss Jenkins safe with me. We had to put the plane down, but she's fine. She's at my cabin."

"Oh, thank goodness, Russ," Mr. Brewer replied. "We were worried sick when you didn't show up ahead of the storm. Is the plane okay?"

"Shattered windshield," Russ replied. "And now everything will be wet. But it could be worse."

"For sure," Brewer agreed. "Okay, now that I know Riley is safe, I'll go home. It's miserable here and getting worse by the minute. My wife will have my hide if I ding the truck."

"Okay," Russ agreed. "Talk to you later."

"Later." As the other man hung up, Russ could have sworn he heard a chuckle.

"Small towns," Russ snorted to himself.

"What was that?" a soft feminine voice broke into his thoughts and he turned to see Riley, standing uncertainly before him. He approached before she could make up her mind to cross that last distance. He took advantage of the moment, wrapping his arms around her waist.

"Riley," he said softly, letting a hint of the bear rumble in his voice.

"What are you doing, Russell?" she asked.

"You know," he said. "You let me kiss you in the dream. What will you let me do here?"

Riley licked her lips and looked through her eyelashes again, shy, but not resistant.

"Keep looking at me like that," he said, "and you're *going to* find yourself kissed."

She made no move to protest or encourage him, so Russ just kissed her. She tasted so sweet, her lips tangy like peaches, soft and plump. She pushed them a bit outward, which he took as a sign of acceptance. Her sweet, feminine scent filled his nostrils, awakening his bear. A roar of triumph vibrated his throat.

He pulled her closer, plastering her body against his, and then snarled. "Your clothes are soaking wet."

"I know," Riley replied.

"Let me get you something. Come with me." Russ took Riley's hand and led her into his bedroom, where he dug around in his drawer and pulled out a sweatshirt. "I don't think I have any pants that will fit you. You're too short. But this would probably cover you to the knees." He handed her the bright green garment.

"Too short?" She cocked an eyebrow at him.

"Only to wear my clothes," he amended. "For everything else, you're perfect."

She smiled.

"Are you socks wet?" Russ continued, eyeing her messy-looking loafers.

"Drenched," she admitted with a grimace. He added some plaid bed socks Mrs. Tomei had knitted.

"I'm going to look like an idiot in this," Riley complained.

"No one will see but me," Russ reminded her. "And you saw me bare-ass naked. Which is worse?"

"Good point."

"I'll go light a fire in the fireplace," he informed her. "I think we might lose power. I want to be ready."

"Okay," Riley agreed. "My first winter in Alaska is turning out to be quite an adventure."

"The adventure is only beginning, honey," he shot back. Then, before he left her to change, he took advantage of her receptive state to kiss her once more. She slipped her arms around his neck. "Hurry, Riley."

"Are we going somewhere?" she quipped.

"I thought dinner and a movie, maybe." She giggled. "But seriously, I want to talk to you, and I don't want to wait anymore."

Her smile faded to consideration. "Okay, Russ. I'll be out in a few minutes." She hugged him gently and then let him go.

Glad for the distraction from thinking about Riley stripping off her school clothes and wondering what kind of panties she wore, he turned his attention to the fireplace. A good supply of dried wood sat on the hearth, next to a hanging collection of fire irons. Long-handled matches awaited him in the drawer of the end table. He quickly assembled the logs and kindling before setting a match to them. Then he stared into the flames, contemplating the dancing orange and gold as though they held the key to the perplexing puzzle that was Riley Jenkins.

She emerged from the bedroom and joined him, sinking to the floor and stroking the thick white fur of an irregularly shaped area rug.

"Is this one of your kind?" she asked.

Russ nodded. "It was one hell of a fight. I didn't want to kill, but he wouldn't stop.

Wouldn't back down. If he'd won, I'd be a decoration in front of his fireplace now."

She shook her head. "Bears are different."

"Yes, and I'm man and bear, which is different again. I wonder how it is that you're so able to accept this." He covered her hand with his.

She shrugged. "I'm still considering whether hysterics would be more appropriate, but I feel the moment for freaking out has passed."

"You're amazing," he told her. He tugged her hand, moving her closer to him. She turned partway, her face in profile to the fire. He also turned, meeting her pretty eyes and wishing the words to say all that hung between them were easier to form. He inhaled her fragrance. So many complex scents. Shampoo, a touch of perfume, and the swirling mélange that seemed to sink into every pore of his body and deep into his soul. He knew what it meant, though he'd never experienced it before. But how could he tell her? How could he phrase all he was thinking and feeling into human terms she would understand, let alone accept? "Riley, I..." he broke off, not sure how to start.

She considered him, biting her lower lip. Then Riley rose up on her knees and leaned forward, touching her lips to his for the briefest of moments before sitting back down in a fiery blush.

Russ couldn't help smiling. "Thank you, Riley. That helped a lot. I guess there's no need to deny there's something between us. Something special."

She nodded, but didn't speak.

"I feel like... it could or maybe should be something more. What do you think?"

She regarded him in silence for a long moment. It took all of Russ' force of will not to interrupt her and press for an answer, but he persevered.

"Are you sure people won't look at us funny?" she said at last.

Russ chuckled. "Honey, this is Alaska, not to mention a very small and remote part of the state. Will people look? Of course. New couples give everyone something to talk about for a few days. But no one will mind. Honestly, they've been speculating about how long it would take us to get together since the day I took out to dinner. No one will be surprised."

"Does anyone know about the bear thing?" she asked.

"Not that I'm aware of," he replied. "No one has called the zookeepers yet, at any rate."

A ghost of a smile creased her lips. "But you look… so much older. I didn't think an older man would be my thing." She looked down, her face a mask of confusion.

"Correct me if I'm wrong, but you don't seem to have much of a 'thing' yet, Riley. Have you had many serious relationships?"

She shook her head.

"How old are you, honey?"

She glanced shyly through her lashes again in a way that made him want to kiss her even more. "Twenty-four." Then she steeled herself. "What about you? At a guess, I'd say you're about forty. No one is going to blink at a sixteen year age difference?" Then her eyes narrowed. "Wait, does the bear thing change your lifespan."

Russ nodded slowly. "It does. While you're not wrong that I'm in early middle age, that doesn't translate to forty years. Though it's sort of equivalent to it."

"How long will you live?" Riley asked, eyes widening.

Russ sighed and lifted Riley's hand to his lips. "Some live to be a hundred-fifty, though it's rare. One-twenty, one-twenty-five. Something like that. I'm sixty-five now. I should have another sixty years or so."

He could see her turning the numbers over in her mind. "That actually kinda works out, doesn't it?"

A slow smile spread across Russ' face. "Pretty well, yes. Riley, I honestly don't think anyone will care about our perceived age difference. Most likely they'll just be happy for us. The question is, if you want to be with me, and I want to be with you, who cares what anyone else thinks?"

"I know, I know," she replied, exhaling loudly. "It's just… it's a small community. I'd like to find a place in it."

"You'll do better at that if you're dating a local," he pointed out. "People will warm up to you more if they know you won't leave at the end of the school year."

She smiled. "There's that."

"So what do you say, Riley? Can we... be a couple?" The words bothered him. They sounded weak and tepid compared to what he wanted to say, but he knew she wasn't ready to hear the rest. This was as good a start as they were likely to get.

"What would that mean, exactly?" she asked. He crooked one eyebrow. "I mean," she amended, "is there some kind of werebear courtship ritual I should know about?"

"Kind of," he replied. "But that's not for today. Down the road a ways, we can talk about it. For now, it would be just what you'd expect. Of course, I'm still flying you from one school to another. That won't change. But when you're not working, we would spend time together. Fly to Fairbanks for a movie or to go shopping. Have dinner at the café. Go for walks in the woods, weather permitting." He laced his fingers through hers. "Touch." Then he drew her nearer to him. "Kiss." He laid his lips on hers for an embrace of ephemeral lightness. "More when you're ready."

He kissed her again. This time more forcefully. This time Russ dared to touch Riley's lips with is tongue. She inhaled sharply. "Let me in, sweet girl," he pleaded.

Riley made a small, inarticulate sound and parted her lips. Russ plunged his tongue into her mouth. He drew her up to her knees so they could press their bodies together. With one hand he cradled the back of her head. The other he splayed on the center of her back. The way her own arms clung to his neck told him she liked how he was touching her, even though she merely acquiesced to the kiss without participating. *Shy baby. I'll teach you.* The thought of tutoring her in every aspect of lovemaking hardened him to aching alertness.

Down, boy. It's going to be a while before you get any action from this shy girl. Enjoy the kiss and don't push her.

Russ teased Riley's tongue with his, plunging into her mouth and retreating, urging her to follow. At last, she made a tentative advance, slipping past his lips. He rewarded her with a lush twirling and tangling that left her gasping. Then he released her from his embrace and helped her to her feet.

"Are you hungry?" he asked.

She studied him, a question lingering in her eyes.

"What is it, Riley?"

"Why did you stop?" The question turned to worry. Though Russ never tried to read anyone's mind, her thoughts were so loud he couldn't prevent them from reaching him. *Did I do it wrong? Why can't I do anything right? Why am I such a baby?*

He stepped back to her, right up against her body and cupped her face in his hand, his palm on her jaw, fingers lacing into the back of her hair. His lips caressed hers once more, gently and without any probing. "I don't want to push you," he said. "I know… I can tell you haven't done a whole lot of this before, and you've taken in a lot today. I thought you might want to take things a bit slowly."

He wrapped his free arm around her waist and urged her head onto his upper chest. *She doesn't even reach my shoulder.*

"Oh," she replied, snuggling closer. "I don't know whether I want to go slowly or not. I've never been in this kind of situation. Would you think less of me if I didn't?"

Her words made no sense when added to everything he knew about her, but they tasted sincere.

"Riley, listen." He arched his hips, pressing the rigid length of his erection into her belly. Even through his clothes and hers the contact caused a wave of pleasure to swell over him. "I want you. I'm not holding back because I have doubts. My bear.... Well, if he had his way, I'd be mating you on the rug right now. He's begging for it." *And I know things about us you're not ready to hear. Things that just might explain why you're so eager.*

She pulled back a step and lifted her eyes to his. Passion, curiosity and a hint of fear swirled in the whiskey-colored depths, raising the already intoxicating effect of her gaze to nearly irresistible. Her cheeks had turned pink, but not a fiery, embarrassed red. Instead the soft glow clearly had been generated by her own passion and desire. His body ached to claim her. With every second he could see the image more clearly, of Riley on hands and knees on the bearskin before the fire, receiving his thick, swollen sex. He stepped back, breaking the spell.

"Decide," he urged. "You have to think about what you want, Riley. I don't want you to have any regrets. Let's make some food. It will give you a chance to work through it. If you want me, you'll have to tell me you do, not that you aren't sure."

She slipped her fingers into his. "You don't ask much, do you?" she quipped. "Make the shy girl ask her..." she blinked and a look of awe spread over her face, "her boyfriend to make love to her." The words, it seemed, tasted as sweet as maple candy. Russ brushed her hair back from her face and stroked her cheek with his thumb. "You know what I want," she added.

I do. I can smell your desire so strongly, I can almost taste it. Your body is ready, but I need to be sure of your mind. "In this world, in this age, love, a man has to hear the words. Assuming anything can lead to trouble."

She acknowledged the truth of his statement by casting her eyes downward and studying the grain of the wood floor.

Russ hugged her for another moment and then released her, heading into his kitchen, which was only separated from the rest of the room by a pine and black granite peninsula. He rummaged in the cabinets and brought to light an enormous frying pan, which he set on one of his stove's six burners.

He dribbled oil into the pan and then turned to the refrigerator.

"This is a nice kitchen," Riley commented. "Much prettier than mine. Do you cook a lot, Russ?"

"I do," he replied. "Since there's only one restaurant in Golden and I don't fly to Fairbanks but about once a month, I eat at home most of the time." Retrieving a foil-wrapped packet, he began to open the crimped metal. "Can you peel some potatoes, please? There's a pot in the cabinet in front of you. Peeler in the drawer above the cabinet."

"Sure thing," Riley agreed cheerfully. "So what are we having?"

"Venison steaks and mashed potatoes," he replied. "Do you like venison? You're not a vegetarian, are you?"

"Not at all," Riley replied. "I've never tried venison. Are you a big hunter then?" He could hear her banging pots and pans as she spoke. The drawer slammed.

"Yes, that I will admit to. Like most bears, I'm happy to eat whatever comes to me, but I have a bit of an advantage for hunting. I don't need a permit."

"Because you're Native Alaskan?" she guessed. "You are, right?"

"Yes," he replied. "Well half."

"And the other half?" she asked, conversationally. "I mean, is the bear thing related to being Native, or is it separate?"

"Curious, aren't you?" he asked as he sprinkled sea salt on the upper sides of the raw meat.

"Of course. Shouldn't I be?" she retorted. "You're my boyfriend, right? So I need to know things about you."

He wanted to hug her, but he had meat juice on his fingers, so he settled for a grin. "Promise you won't sell me to the zoo?" he quipped.

"I don't think so," she replied with a teasing smirk.

"I just can't get over," he added as he flipped the steaks and sprinkled seasoning on the bottoms. *Now let them come to room temperature,* "how easily you accepted this."

"I know, right?" Riley replied, slicing one potato and slipping it into a pot of water before turning to the next one. "Three okay?"

"Better do five," Russ replied. "I have a high metabolism."

"Okay."

"So..." he pondered how to start. "Let me tell you a story that was told to me when I was a youth."

At her nod, he continued.

"In ancient times, long before humans walked across the ice to this place, the bears were kings and queens of this land. They played and hunted in the forests. One night, the bear goddess looked down from the sky – you know of the bear goddess, do you not?"

She considered. "I know the constellation of Ursa Major."

"That's the one. Anyway, she and her cub came down to earth. While the star cub played with the other baby bears, the goddess found the biggest and strongest of the boar bears and took him as her lover. And in the winter, when the wind howled over the earth and the snow lay deep on the ground, she returned with three newborn cubs, which she left with a kind sow bear whose own cubs had died."

Russell glanced at Riley. She had all the potatoes cut and in the water. He set the pot on the stove and cranked the fire to high, adding a liberal pinch of his sea salt.

"The three cubs soon realized that they, like their goddess mother, could change forms at will, and they mimicked all the creatures in the forest. They also had self-awareness a normal bear does not possess. They were sentient, intelligent, shape-shifting bears.

"Later, humans came to this area, the Den'a, whom anthropologists call Athabaskans. The shifter bears had bred with normal bears over many generations, and the gene pool was getting a bit thin, but the shifters realized these humans were more like them: Sentient, thinking creatures. So they took their form and began to interact with them. Most of the Den'a family groups feared these white-haired strangers and ran from them. Only one small family, isolated from the others, welcomed them. They had the strongest Shaman tradition of all the groups, which fit in well with the idea of bears that could become human. Over time, an arrangement was made whereby each generation a human from among the Den'a and a bear shifter would mate, to infuse fresh blood into the communities." He stopped, a bit lost in his story.

"So is that what you mean by half? Half Den'a, half shifter?"

Russell nodded. "Leave it to you, Riley, to see exactly what I mean. My father is a holy man in the village. He also has shifter blood, as did his father. It has become a family legacy. The village is still a tiny and isolated community. You won't have any of my cousins in your class. We have developed a distinct culture and even a separate language from the rest of the Athabaskans. Interestingly, this blending of blood also affects the bear gene. Once human blood entered the shifters' line, they could only turn into humans and bears. The other animal forms were lost."

"How interesting," Riley replied. She fell silent and Russ could practically see the gears turning in her head.

“Would you set the table, please?” he asked, opening the cabinet above them and wondering how she would react to dishes that looked like they were made of wood. She met his eyes and smiled. *Typical Riley. She seems able to absorb anything I throw at her.* He stirred the potatoes and rummaged in the fridge for milk. The butter and potato masher waited on the counter.

She set plates at the table, and then with another questioning glance, rooted around until she found cups, forks and steak knives. He waited for his territorial bear to rise and start growling, but it didn’t. *Apparently, he trusts her.*

And the man Russell trusted her too. It transcended any rational explanation. He simply knew, without a doubt, that Riley was the one.

Russell stirred the potatoes again, adjusting the heat to be sure they didn’t boil over. Washing starchy water from the stove drove him nuts. He turned the heat on under the oily skillet. Then he turned to see Riley standing beside the bay window opposite the fireplace, staring out into the swirling snow. Russell approached and wrapped his arms around her waist. He rested his chin on the top of her head.

"It's so peaceful out there. Pure and white," she said in a soft, wistful voice. "It feels like nothing bad could ever touch me here."

"You have a guardian of more than usual strength," he replied. Her shampoo teased his nose with a soft floral scent.

"So it would seem. Am I truly safe, Russell?"

He kissed her hair. "Yes, love. There's a whole lot of teeth and claws between you and any bullying older brother."

"If only you could defend me against memories."

Russell tightened his arms around her. "Then we should make some new memories. How does that sound? Let the bad ones float away. Send them into the snow, never to be seen again. Keep the ones that make you happy. And we'll add to that list."

Riley turned in his embrace, her luminous eyes glowing. "How can I feel so much so fast?" she asked. "We've barely met."

"Every relationship starts somewhere," he replied. "Even the ones that last a lifetime were once new."

"Is that how you see this?" she asked, and he could tell that this question, at least, was not idle.

"I do," he said, in his most serious tone. "But why worry about lifetimes now? Let's enjoy being in a brand new and very promising relationship. What do you say?"

"Yes," she answered simply, just as the timer on the stove chimed.

"Hold that thought." Russ kissed the end of Riley's nose before hurrying back to slap the two small steaks in the pan, where they hissed loudly. A tantalizing aroma of cooking meat spread through the cabin.

Riley jumped into action, draining the potatoes and mashing them with the ingredients he'd set out. *How nice to have a helper.* It allowed him time to open a can of beans and heat them up as well.

A moment later he dished up two plates of food, steaming hot and fragrant. Riley eyed the feast hungrily.

"Wine?" he asked, and she agreed with a shrug and a nod.

Russ poured two glasses of Shiraz and joined Riley at the table. "Sure you're legal?" he quipped.

She giggled and pushed on his shoulder. "Quit teasing, old man." They both laughed, then they applied themselves to their dinner.

Riley, Russ noted, ate with intense concentration, as though every forkful of food meant so much more than mere sustenance. He sipped his wine as he watched her eat, his own food forgotten on his plate. *Eat, man. You do have it bad, don't you?* Shaking off rumination, he began to work on his own meal, but his eyes wanted to stray across Riley's curves. Her breasts curved under the front of his sweatshirt, practically begging to be touched, and the sight of her slender legs, bare from mid-thigh to mid-calf, would remain forever etched in his memory. The girl captivated him, from the curve of her jaw to the delicately pulsing artery in her neck, her dainty collarbone, her narrow waist. *She's the real feast here.* Riley lifted her eyes from her plate and caught him staring at her. Her face pinkened. Then she shocked him by reaching across the table and stroking the stubble on his cheek.

“The food is delicious, Russell,” she commented. “Thank you.”

He set down his fork so he could capture her hand and lifted it to his lips. “I needed to be sure my sweet lady was well cared for,” he replied, enjoying the darkening color of her cheeks. “Have you had enough?” He indicated her plate, where most of the food had disappeared.

“Yes, thank you,” she replied. “It was so good.”

Russell’s own plate was not nearly as empty as usual, but his stomach no longer growled, so he scraped the remnants into the trash and rinsed the dishes before tucking them into the dishwasher. Riley followed suit.

Tasks complete, they stopped dead in the middle of the kitchen, staring at each other. Riley’s lower lip found its way between her teeth. She looked so heart-meltingly uncertain. “What is it?” Russell asked.

“I. . . ” her pale face darkened to scarlet and she broke eye contact, lowering her gaze to the floor.

Russ closed the distance between them in an instant, gathering her close. “What is it, Riley,” he murmured into her ear.

Riley slipped her arms around his neck and laid her cheek on his chest. *She wants a hug? That's easy enough.* Warming her in his embrace, Russell took in her scent again. Something nervous and embarrassed had wormed its way in, as well as an anticipation that stole his breath and made his heart pound. *She knows what she wants. She just doesn't know how to say it.*

Reasoning that she could always stop him, he released the hug and guided her across the open floor of the cabin to a wide leather armchair facing the fireplace. He sank down on the comfortable surface and pulled her onto his lap. One big, rugged and calloused hand cupped her face, drawing her close. His lips trailed across her cheek, seeking her lips and then claiming them in a lush, open-mouthed kiss.

"Do you want this?" he projected into her mind as his tongue plunged between her lips. The intimate contact seemed to thaw her nervous stiffness. Her shoulders relaxed and her body molded itself into the unyielding wall of his torso.

"I want you," she replied without speaking, but must have known he would hear her. The targeted thought could only have been deliberate.

"And you have me," he sent back, confirming her message had been received. She inhaled sharply. "And I have you. This is meant to be Riley. We're meant to claim each other."

Shyly, her tongue crept to his and touched. The love play of the kiss increased in heat and tempo as they took turns possessing each other's mouths. Russ coaxed Riley to enter and rewarded her with a teasing lick. With one hand he still held her face, keeping her a willing captive to his embrace. With the other, he stroked her back up and down. Riley clung to his shoulders as though to a lifeline. *She's drowning in desire already, from only a kiss.* Pressing, testing the limits of her willingness, he slipped his hand around her body and laid it flat on her belly. The small outward curve fluttered under his touch. She seemed to sense that the moment was poised on a razor's edge. Whether he moved up or down, she would be forever changed. For a moment her body tensed, and then the tension melted like snow in sunshine, pooling in liquid desire he could smell as well as sense. In passion, her scent grew even more enticing. His bear urged action, as did his sex, which ached with readiness, hard and throbbing with the need to plunge into her. Rational man fought with ancient instinct. *I can't hold out long. I need her too much.* Deliberately he moved upward, cupping the softness of one breast.

Riley captured Russ' lower lip and nibbled, seeming to desire a distraction from his first intimate touch. He allowed the move. *Slow and easy, baby girl. Take it at your own pace.* She made no move to pull back from his exploration, however, and her nipple welcomed him, rising to touch his palm. He thumbed the peak and was rewarded with a wave of pleasure he could feel radiating from her. Her kiss turned desperate. He let her ravage his mouth, but still his fingers stroked and played over the tender tip of her breast. He could feel how much she liked his touch, but her mind had awakened and was nervous.

"So sweet," he murmured against her lips. Then, in a slow, deliberate movement, he fisted the fabric of her sweatshirt and lifted it high, raising his head so he could see what he had been touching. Round, upright globes of medium size tantalized him with cherry pink nipples set in smooth, pale skin. Despite the fire, the coolness in the room quickly teased the peaks even more erect. They seemed to beg for his attention. Russ reached for the as-yet unstimulated breast, but Riley stayed his hand with a soft touch of her fingertips.

With a gulp, she moved of her own accord, lifting the sweatshirt over her head and tossing it aside.

Now clad only in a pair of blue lace panties and his funny knitted socks, she lifted her head defiantly, daring him to comment.

"You're gorgeous, Riley," he said, running gentle fingers down her shoulder and arm to her hand, where he laced their fingers together. "Beautiful and brave. I'm so glad you're mine."

She closed her eyes, thick dark lashes sweeping her cheeks. He touched his lips to her eyebrow.

"May I touch you some more? I want to make you feel good."

Her eyes flew open and she inhaled a slow, deep breath. Though it seemed her words had abandoned her, her body acquiesced to his request, back arching to offer her breasts to his touch. Not wanting to torture her with anticipation, he took her invitation immediately, cupping the soft fullness and stroking the silky skin. This time, he lowered his head and kissed her nipple, then glanced up to gauge her reaction. She seemed to be considering, so he opened and delivered a gentle suck.

This time Riley's gasp was one of pure, startled pleasure. Her fingers laced into his hair, holding him right where she wanted him. He licked and nibbled one nipple, stroked and tugged the other. Riley emitted a soft moan. Russell smiled against her breast. Once again, uncertainty had faded to acquiescence. He released her and indulged in another long look. Her lips were slightly parted, her intoxicating eyes hazy. Her nipples glistened in the firelight. Her breath came in little pants. *She's almost ready already. Time to take her to another level.* His bear protested with an almost audible roar. *Soon, buddy. You won't regret the wait.*

Russell cupped Riley's panties, laying his hand flat on her mound. Her passion tears had soaked the fabric. He deliberately moved the scrap of lace to the side, baring her completely to his touch.

"Russ!" she gasped. Then her inhalation faded to a moan as he ran two fingers up and down her slick folds, anointing them with her juices in preparation for an even more intimate touch.

"I want to give you pleasure, Riley. Will you let me? Should I stop?" Even as he asked the question, he pushed one finger into the opening of her body and was unsurprised to find his passage partially blocked. "Why, Riley, are you a virgin?" he teased.

"Not..." she sucked air into her lungs. "Not for much longer. Don't stop, Russ." Deliberately she spread her thighs.

Humbled by her trust, Russell set out to bring his lady as much pleasure as he could. His aimless stroking soon settled in on her clitoris and he set out to make Riley feel good by moving the swollen nub in a slow circle.

Her moans changed to whimpers and even more moisture slicked her folds. "Your body wants me, little girl," he told her.

Her response was somewhat less than coherent.

Recalling how tight and unyielding her innocent passage had been, Russ changed his motion, working her clit with this thumb so he could open her with his fingers. Slowly he inserted one again, and the clinging wetness nearly broke his control. Bear and man wanted into that tiny well with equal fervency. Determined to give Riley the best possible awakening, he grimly fought down his own urges. First she clenched against his invasion, but gradually her body acclimated. Another whimpering sob escaped her. This time he pressed two fingers into her well, pushing right to the barrier that denied him full access to her body. Easing his fingers in and out in a gentle imitation of intercourse, he worked her clitoris with his thumb and waited. Riley's every breath caught on a sob as her peak neared. Soon she would be writhing in his arms. *Soon… soon… soon…* NOW.

Riley cried out sweetly as her body reacted. Her sex clamped down on his fingers and her clit throbbed under his thumb. Every muscle locked and trembled as her pleasure peaked. Russell looked on in approval as his lady enjoyed her orgasm. Gently he eased his fingers deeper until he once again encountered her barrier. Allowing one claw to extend, he punctured the membrane. *That will help with what's to come.* And as he hoped, she seemed not to notice. Long moments passed as Riley squirmed in ecstasy, but at last she fell limp, her cheek on his shoulder. He kissed her hair again.

"Feel good?" he asked, unable to conceal completely the rumble in his voice. His bear would not be denied much longer. *Time to move while I still have control.*

"Mmmmm," she answered in a wordless hum. He grinned. *Speechless. Not bad.*

Russ tucked one finger under Riley's chin and lifted her face, kissing her back to awareness.

"Your turn?" she asked sweetly, though she looked a bit nervous now.

"My turn," he agreed. "Now, earlier, you asked me if there were any bear courtship rituals you should know about. There is one." He set her on her feet and walked her over to the rug in front of the fireplace. She watched in unabashed curiosity as he stripped off his sweater and pants.

Swallowing hard, Riley shimmied her panties down her legs, taking the socks along, so she stood nude before him. "What would that be?"

Russ couldn't tear his eyes off the vision of feminine beauty before him. Though petite and slender, Riley was still no stick figure. Softly curving breasts, belly, hips and thighs graced her frame. *Mine!* Man and bear snarled together. He stepped close, pulling her into his arms for a tender kiss. He sank to his knees, drawing her with him, but then instead of lowering her to her back, he turned her away from him.

"The first time we have sex, it has to be in this position," he told her, urging her forward.

She turned to look over her shoulder. "This time?"

"Yes, only this time. After that, I plan to try out every position there is with you, Riley. Is that okay?"

"Uh..." the corners of her eyes tightened. "Let's get this one done first."

"Right. Sorry, sweetheart. I'm not really myself right now. I want you so bad. Are you okay?"

"I feel very... exposed," she replied. "Russ, before I chicken out, you should probably hurry."

Russell laid his hand on her hip, stroking to soothe her. He understood why she felt exposed. Every inch of her glistening sex lay bare for his perusal. Her clitoris stood proud and dark against the pink folds. He couldn't help but touch it again. Riley gasped. "Muh… more?" she stammered.

"Do you think I'll ever get tired of watching you come? I don't," he replied. It took every ounce of willpower Russ possessed to pleasure Riley once more. He penetrated her with one and then two fingers, but without the barrier of her hymen, he was able to enter her fully, preparing her to receive what he was aching to give her. So soon after her last climax, he was able to bring her to pleasure quickly. Within a few short moments, her hips were rocking and her body clenching as ecstasy swept her. Russell withdrew his fingers. Grasping his erection with one hand, he lined it up with her opening. Despite his preparations, she still seemed impossibly tiny. She sucked air through her teeth and her body tensed, but Russ didn't retreat. A sharp nudge pushed the crown of his sex into her. Another nudge and the head disappeared.

He couldn't tear his eyes away from the sight of their bodies slowly merging. Riley gasped and hissed but never protested. With short, gentle thrusts, Russell progressed deeper and deeper until, after what seemed like an eternity, he had filled her completely. Her depth matched him well, and the sensation of wet, throbbing heat caressed him with the most indescribable pleasure. Unable to contain himself, Russell threw back his head. The bear roared in triumph, forcing an ursine bellow through his human throat.

Not much time remained to Russ to enjoy mating his woman. He had waited too long. But he did take a moment to cover Riley, laying his chest fully against her back, the way a bear would do. In a soft undertone, he articulated words ancient beyond human measurement. Then he lifted his body upright and grasped Riley's hips in his hands. "All right, love. You're doing so well, and I'm almost there. Are you hurting?"

"No," she replied. "It feels strange. So big. But not painful."

"Good. How about this?" He pulled back and pushed again. She squeaked. "That all right?"

"Yes, Russell. It doesn't hurt."

Reassured, he began to move slowly in and out of her tight passage. There was no room for harder thrusting, but for today, this gentle loving would more than suffice.

Riley lowered herself to her elbows, her cheek on the rug, eyes closed. The movement caused a ripple to caress him. Beads of sweat broke out on Russ' forehead. His canines lengthened. He had to fight to keep his fingers human enough to hold her without scratching her.

Quickly now, no time to waste, Russell thrust, groaning, daring to take Riley a little harder. Another roar was ripped from his mouth as his pleasure peaked. Hot seed spilled deep in Riley. He growled words that had never belonged to human language. Words she could never understand.

When the spasm finally faded, Russell eased out of Riley's body and laid her on her side, curling up behind her. "I'm sorry," he said. "I lost control. You felt so good."

"Don't be sorry," she urged. "It was… very nice. You made me feel good also."

"I'm glad," he said. "You're an amazing girl, Riley. I'm so happy you're mine."

"And I'm happy you're mine." She rolled over in his arms. "So happy."

They gazed into each other's eyes with expressions of mutual adoration. Russ didn't dare say all that was in his heart. Not yet. But for now it was enough to know that they were together, and that they were one.

Chapter 5

Russell opened his eyes with a start. His shoulder ached and his back felt tremendously cold. Deep darkness seemed to close in all around him. *What's going on*? Instantly on the alert, Russell stretched out with his other senses. He could hear nothing, and there was something disturbing about the silence. It seemed wrong. He could smell nothing out of the ordinary, though with the sweet aroma of woman and flowers bathing the entire scentscape, he couldn't quite tell. *Wait, woman… flowers? Riley!* Ah yes. Her comforting softness pressed against the front of his body. Beneath them, he recognized the fur rug. *I'm lying on the great room floor in front of the fireplace.* Being able to pinpoint his location helped Russ understand more. The scent of Riley barely concealed the lingering smokiness of a cold fireplace. The fire had gone out. So had the power, which was why the silence sounded wrong. The hiss of the heater and the hum of the refrigerator rarely registered on his senses, but their absence did.

Sagging with relief, Russell slipped away from Riley's body, flipping the edge of the rug over her to keep her warm. Working largely by touch, he placed several logs and some kindling into the fireplace. As he stirred the ashes, he found a few live coals, which glowed red as the air teased them. The faint illumination showed him where to touch a rolled up newspaper. The chilly bricks of the hearth seemed to bite at his bare skin as he breathed on the paper and the coal, and he sighed in relief as flame flared. He quickly touched it to the kindling, which caught instantly, licking upward against the larger logs.

It would be a while before the fire sufficed to warm the house, and Russell didn't feel like waiting naked in the cold. He moved the rug away from Riley and carefully lifted her. She didn't weigh nearly enough to tax his ursine strength, and he easily carried her through the dimly lit living room and into his bedroom. She stirred, making a sleepy sound that turned his heart over, and she snuggled into his chest.

He eased her under the quilt and followed her. The chill of the sheets assaulted them both and Riley rocketed upright, nearly taking out Russell's nose.

"Easy, honey," he said in a low rumble. "I just moved us to the bed. Everything's okay."

"Russell?" she sounded confused.

"Yes, honey. I'm right here. The power is out, but I have a fire going, and now that we're under the blankets, we should warm up soon."

She settled back down against the pillow, drawing as close to him as she could get, her head on his shoulder, her knee on his belly.

Russell smiled. Snowed in, power out and he couldn't be happier. Content, he closed his eyes.

* * *

Russell sat up in his bed, but he knew he was dreaming. Riley sat beside him, her legs drawn up to her chest, arms wrapped around her knees. Russell extended his hand. She grasped it.

"This is interesting," he said.

"What is?" Her whiskey dark eyes seemed to glow in the dim bedroom.

"I didn't have to invite you into my dream. You were just here."

"Maybe it's my dream," she suggested in that saucy way she had.

Russell snorted. "Sure, Riley. Most likely it's our dream."

"I didn't know that was a real thing, sharing dreams," Riley said, and he could see how puzzled she had become. "I thought all those times I dreamed about you, it was just because I had a crush..."

"One that was enthusiastically returned," he replied. Watching the questioning frown on her forehead and lips turn to a smile delighted him. "So I'm pretty sure you were sleeping before me. What were you doing, just waiting here?"

Riley shook her head. "I was outside. The stars were... whispering to me? I don't know. It seemed like they were. And the Big Dipper... I saw it and it got bigger, brighter. It seemed to pulse and glow at me. I couldn't stop looking at it. Russell, what does it mean?"

"It means you were blessed by the Sky Bear," Russell replied, awed. "You can't imagine how special that is. To the best of my knowledge, only the Den'a have received her favor thus far."

"The Sky Bear? Why would she bless me, Russell?"

"I think I know."

"Is this a shape shifter thing?" she asked, suspicious.

"Of course," he admitted. "Have you had enough shape shifter things? We don't have to talk about everything at once."

Riley climbed into his lap. He looped his arms around her.

"Russell, in the past day, I've crash landed in your airplane..."

"Wait a minute," he interrupted, "that was an emergency landing, not a crash."

"Okay, okay, Mr. Precise." She rolled her eyes. "I 'emergency landed' in a plane with a tree in it, nearly froze to death, watched my crush turn into a bear and had sex for the first time. I think, if I'm not freaking out by now, a story isn't going to do it."

"You're something else, Riley," he commented. "Okay." Her scent tickled his awareness. "You know how they say animals can smell intentions, more or less?"

"Yes," she said, her face twisting as she tried to wrap her mind around his non sequitur.

"It's not exactly that, but kind of. Scent, body language and a few other, less easily defined traits make it possible for animals to know a person's motivations sometimes before they do." He paused, wondering where to go next. "There are parts of me that remain a bear even when I'm in human form. Some of my senses – smell and hearing for instance. And my appetite. And there are parts of me that stay human even when I'm in bear form, such as my intellect and reasoning ability. Okay?"

"Yeah, I can see that," she replied.

"Right. Well, part of that means I have greater than average intuition about people. From the first time we met, I knew things about you."

"Like what?" Now Riley looked a bit concerned. He kissed her hand.

"Like how kind you are. How much you want to help your students, even when they drive you crazy. I knew you were afraid of something, and I knew you got over being afraid of me really quickly. I knew you were shy, but underneath it, also intelligent and funny. I knew those things within the first week. I knew in the first moment that you would never seek to cause harm to me or anyone else."

"Wow." Riley blinked. "I think you have a higher opinion of me than I do of myself."

"I'm sure of it," Russ replied. "It doesn't matter what *he* told you about your worth. You know he was crazy, so don't pay it any mind."

The oblique reference to her brother elicited a shiver from deep within Riley's frame. "Let's not go there. So all this is very interesting, but I'm not sure how it applies. You knew I was an okay person and that's why we feel this attraction so strongly?"

"Yes and no," he said. "Okay, so part of me is always bear, and part of me is always human. But there are a few things about me that are uniquely shifter. This is going to sound crazy..." Riley raised one eyebrow at him. "Okay, perhaps a bit crazier than anything to date." The second eyebrow joined the first and her eyes widened. "A shifter is unique because we can smell our mate. I'm not sure exactly how it works, whether it's some kind of fate, biology or a combination of the two. There haven't been studies done of shifters, but it's a fact. I can say now that I've experienced it. At a guess I'd say the scent of the person whose DNA perfectly complements our own creates a flood of neurotransmitters that cause an instant and unbreakable bond."

"So it's not love at first sight but love at first scent?" Riley quipped.

Russ nodded. "That's it exactly. At first, I wasn't sure what I was feeling. I had heard of 'scenting' one's mate before, but I thought it was a shifter myth, like the Sky Bear one I told you the other day. This one at least is apparently true. Because the first time you climbed into my plane, I knew we would be good together, and that I wanted to be with you."

"Wow," she breathed. "So what does that mean for us, Russell?"

Russ traced Riley's cheekbone with one fingertip. "It means I'm committed to you, to this relationship. The more time I spend with you, the better I like you. I don't see that changing anytime soon. But I realize you're human, Riley. That 'just knowing' you belong with someone because of the way they smell isn't going to work for you. You'll need time to know how we fit together, to build up trust and all. That's okay with me, as long as we can be a couple while we work through the process."

"It's a lot to take in," Riley said. "I feel something for you, Russell. It's strong and sweet. I'm attracted to you, have been from the first. And I enjoy spending time with you. I'm glad we're a couple, but you're right. Calling this a fated relationship for life is a bit hard to grasp. What does that mean, exactly? Is it like a marriage?"

"To a certain extent," he replied honestly. "I'm committed to you, as I said. If we were both shifters, no further ceremony would be needed. When shifters find their mate, that's it. They're a couple for life. But like I said, I'll take this slowly."

"You have a different definition of slowly than I do," she said dryly. "It's November and we met in September." Her words were undermined by the twinkle in her eyes.

"Even for a human, becoming a couple after two months isn't that unusual."

"Maybe not agreeing to date," she replied, suddenly serious. "But all this... talking about fate and sleeping together... that's a bit fast."

It wasn't, he knew, but he also didn't want to argue. If it felt fast to her, it was fast. What other people did was irrelevant.

"I'll give you time, sweet girl. I won't rush you. As long as you don't run, you can have all the time you need."

"Russell." Her voice turned fond and her fingertips smoothed the stubble on his cheek. "I have no intention of running away from you. I don't know about fated mates, but I know this relationship is something I want. I care for you. You care for me. So far we've been great as friends. If we're rushing this a bit... that's okay. I trust you."

The sweet words drew him down to her lips. He kissed her with lingering tenderness. She stroked his face while their mouths clung.

"It's going to be fine," he told her. "Wait and see."

"I will," she agreed.

This time, she drew him back down into the kiss, curling her tongue around his. At last, he broke away, gasping. "We should sleep for real, love. Now that I've had you… I'll need you again soon."

She giggled, a blush creeping over her cheeks. "Okay."

He stretched out in the dream bed, mimicking their position in the real world. "Sleep, Riley. I'm here."

She nestled into his arms and they settled into restful slumber.

Chapter 6

Being snowed in over Thanksgiving proved to be so much fun, they made it last as long as they could. Long after the power came back on, they still puttered around Russell's cabin, talking, cooking, and making love. Russ took great pleasure in tutoring Riley to enjoy sex. She proved to be an apt and eager pupil. But at last the time came for them to emerge from their pleasure haze and reconnect with real life. Sunday, Russell showed Riley his oversize garage, where a snowmobile awaited. She eyed the machine nervously.

"I take it you've never ridden before," he suggested.

"Nope," she replied. "And a friend of mine broke his arm on one back in high school." Though her tone was light, her eyes lingered on the chrome and a worried frown creased the skin between her eyebrows.

Russell scooped her into his arms and kissed the crinkle until it smoothed away. "That kid was probably hot-dogging. I'll drive carefully. All you have to do is hold onto me. Can you handle that, Riley?"

She nodded, though she looked far from convinced.

"Come on, you've ridden a wild bear. How much worse can this be?"

"Well, when you put it that way..." Some of the sparkle returned to her eyes. Russell straddled the snowmobile and extended a hand. A moment later Riley's slender curves pressed against his back, her arms gripping tight around his waist.

"Safety first," he said, handing her a helmet with a darkened visor. "Are you warm enough?"

"Not really," she replied, "but I don't want to go back to town in your clothes. They don't fit me. We can stop by my apartment first, and I can change out of school clothes, if that's okay."

"Sure it is, honey," he replied. Then he revved the engine and set the snowmobile in motion. As he zipped between the towering pines, headed toward Golden, the soft speaking of nature was drowned out by the noise of the engine. He preferred walking – as man or bear – but it was too far for Riley, especially now that winter had set in.

Eventually the quiet drone of the engine seemed to lull her, and she relaxed against him, her head pressing into his back. *She still has plenty of adjusting to do before she's truly at home in Alaska.*

Trees opened out into a small meadow with a partially frozen stream. Two deer nibbling the bark of a pine shot their heads into the air and stared at the noisy creature that had just burst upon them. Then they turned as one and sprang into the undergrowth. Russell steered away from the deer, not wanting to alarm them more than necessary.

The snowmobile ate up the miles quickly, and before twenty minutes had passed, the town of Golden appeared on the horizon. First the landscape sprouted up isolated homes like Russell's with increasing frequency. Then outlying subdivisions crowded cheek by jowl in one or two block squares of matching new construction. At last the town proper became visible. A few taller buildings, mostly historic. Some houses. A school. A store. A church. Russell reduced speed. Eventually he skidded to a halt and helped Riley to her feet. She groaned and waddled around, rubbing her aching thighs while he chained the snowmobile to a tree. Then, pocketing the ignition key, he gathered up his girlfriend and walked her into town, arm around her waist.

Though not overly large, Golden had a bit more size than was comfortable to walk in cold weather, and Riley began to shiver in no time. Russ tried to keep her warm, but didn't succeed as well as he would have liked, and by the time they arrived at the former mansion that had been subdivided into rental units, she was stumbling.

Her fingers fumbled and slipped on the security keypad.

"What's the code," he demanded.

She stuttered it out between chattering teeth and he quickly punched the numbers in and then dragged her through the door. Inside a blast of heat belched from radiators at the floor level of the lobby, which had once been a formal living room, though now the wood floors looked scuffed and tired. Russ hauled Riley into his arms, warming her as best he could.

A blast of icy wind bit into him and he cursed as the door swung open. A woman with wild, curly hair stepped over the threshold and tutted.

"She's freezing," he tried to explain, but Riley took the initiative and lifted her head.

"Not a word, Margo," she cautioned, her teasing tone subsumed by chattering teeth. "Want me to tell people what I saw last week?"

"You're evil, Riley," the woman replied, smoothing her mop of black hair out of her eyes. "You might as well get your story ready, because you and Russell Tadzea finally becoming a real couple… I can't hold that back."

"Finally? We've known each other two months," Riley protested. Her shivering had slowed and she seemed steadier on her feet.

"I think… well everyone thinks you two were made for each other. No one will be surprised you succumbed. If there was any way to confirm suspicions… I think they would have taken bets how you two spent your vacation."

Riley's face flamed a brilliant, painful scarlet.

"I think you just confirmed the speculation, honey," Russell pointed out as Margo burst out laughing.

"At any rate," the woman continued. "It's cold in this hallway. I'll see you two love birds later." She breezed out.

"What floor are you on?" Russell asked, trying to distract Riley from the fact that everyone would now know their business.

"Follow me," she replied.

As she led the way up flight after flight of stairs, Russell regarded the ragged wallpaper and droopy, water-stained ceilings with a bit of regret. Back in its heyday this had been one of the nicest addresses in town, the home of a gold tycoon and his family. But once the grandchildren had squandered the last of the money and slouched off to Anchorage, Fairbanks and Nome in search of employment, the place had been let go. Clearly the years had not been kind to the old girl. He supposed Riley could afford better, but in this town, better was not really available at any price.

She drew a key out of her purse and unlocked a door, beckoning to him and staring pointedly at a dangerous hump in the carpet. He stepped over and entered her apartment.

Here, some of the shabbiness had been spruced up with fresh paint and colorful rag rugs covering the stained floor. Though only a small studio, Riley had worked hard to make the place homey with thrift store paintings and colorful dishes in the glass front cabinets opposite the door. A bold red rooster adorned a hand towel hanging from the oven door. A matching ceramic spoon rest brightened the stove top. To the right, a tiny table and two chairs stood between cheap second hand bookshelves groaning with equally cheap second-hand books. To the left, a brass day bed had been left open; a thick white quilt lay crumpled on top. On a table beside the bed/sofa a heavy, leather-framed book sat open, yellowed pages heavily marked with notes in a spidery, slanted hand.

"Nice place," he commented.

"Not compared to your cabin," Riley replied.

"Who's comparing?" Russ asked, moving to examine the book more closely as Riley opened a wardrobe and tossed her crumpled, sink-washed clothes into a laundry basket inside, and then moved naked across the room to rummage in a slender dresser. A minute later, clad in jeans, turtleneck and sweater, with thick, multicolored socks on her feet, she sighed with comfort.

"That's better. I thought I was going to freeze just walking across town."

"It's a real possibility," Russ warned her. "Winter in Alaska is nothing to mess around with." His eyes traveled around the room again. "This is kind of a shitty building. I mean, you've done nice things with the room, but still."

Riley shrugged. "I'm not ready to buy or build a house yet. I think I should work here at least a year and be sure I can stand the town before I make any permanent commitments. Since the only other rental is a five bedroom house I don't need, this will do. What choice do I have?"

Russell slipped his arms around Riley's waist from behind and rested his chin on the top of her head. "You do have an option, you know. My home is always open to you."

She stiffened. "Russ, I… " her words trailed off.

"I know you're not ready to think about it now, honey. But I really did like having you there. If you want to move in, you're more than welcome. There's a place in bed beside me waiting for you."

Riley turned in Russell's arms and looked up into his eyes. "I'll think about that. I mean, seriously think whether it's a good idea. I'm not brushing you off."

"I know you're not, Riley. I understand it's not a decision to make on the fly. I didn't expect you to say yes today."

"I probably will at some point," she admitted, her cheeks pinkening again.

"Just can't get enough, can you?" he teased, just to see that blush grow. Riley didn't disappoint.

"Kiss me, you evil man," she said, half laughing as she drew him down. Russell lingered a long moment with his lips on Riley's. Her taste intoxicated him. Being mated felt fantastic, much better than he would ever have imagined. He was loving every moment.

"Hmmm," he replied, half in a hum, half in an ursine growl of pleasure. "Are you cold?" he teased, running his fingers over her side.

She squeaked and jerked away from him. "Cut that out! No, I'm practically sweating. You're better than a furnace, Russell."

"Good." He kissed her lips. "Are you hungry?"

"I could eat. But I suspect you ask because you are."

He shook his head. "You know me too well, babe." He turned to head toward the door, but his eye was snared again by the massive book sitting open on the table, the text nearly obscured with a spidery scrawl.

"What is this?" he asked, peeking over his shoulder at her.

Riley's smile turned sad. "My only legacy from my father," she replied. "This was one of his favorite books. He quoted it for everything."

Russell gently closed the cover and saw that it was a leather-bound copy of the writings of St. Francis of Assisi.

"Interesting choice," Russell commented.

"My father was a gentle soul," she replied. "It hurt him deeply when he found out my brother had been… doing what he did." She shuddered.

Russ turned and rose, snuggling up against her body. "I'm here, Riley. I'm always here for you. He can't hurt you anymore."

"I know," she replied, though her tone was far from steady.

"And you couldn't have put any greater distance between you, Riley. Not without leaving the country. You saved yourself first. You're strong and brave."

"I'm a mouse and I ran like hell." She regarded him with haunted, regret-filled eyes. "I gave him everything that was mine and I ran away."

"What do you mean?" Russ asked, wishing he could read her mind. Clearly this was something she needed to get off her chest, but he could see her flinching with her desire not to do it. "What did you give him?"

Riley tried to withdraw from his embrace.

"No, honey, don't pull away. I saw your dream, remember. Didn't your brother go to jail?"

Silence stretched out in the tiny studio. Outside, Russ could hear the wind whistling among the buildings, the honks and revving engines of traffic streaming past. "He did," she burst out, as though desperate to get the words said before she lost her nerve. "He served several years for assault... not of me. But eventually he got out. While my father was alive, he kept Danny away from me. But then he died." She sniffled.

"How did he die?" Russell asked kindly. "Was he ill?"

"No," she sucked in a noisy breath. "He had a stroke. He seemed fine when I went home, but the next day he didn't answer his phone. I went to his home... he was lying in bed..." her voice broke, but she muscled on. "Cold and gray. I don't want to remember him as a corpse, Russ."

"Of course not." He stroked her hair. "Was he young? Was it a shock?"

"Not young," she admitted. "He was over fifty when I was born. He lived to be seventy-three. It was a shock, but not completely unexpected. His blood pressure, you know?"

Russell kissed her cheek. "I'm sorry you had to see him that way. So, you told me he was a scholar. Can you remember him like that? With this book in his hands?"

She laughed through a sob. "Yes. I don't have to try hard for that. He carried it everywhere, lost it all the time."

"I can picture it," Russ replied. "Riley, what happened?"

Her shoulders stiffened. "When he... passed, I inherited everything he had," Riley said. "Our house. His car. All his possessions. He left me everything."

He can't have had much, Russell thought. *Scholars are seldom wealthy.*

"It wasn't much," Riley added, confirming his suspicions. "But that house was my childhood home. I was looking forward to living there. The studio I rented after I started teaching didn't measure up. And there was a small nest egg too. But really, I just wanted to go home. I missed him, and I wanted to be in a place that still felt and smelled like him. It was my home, and I wanted to go back, even if he wasn't there."

"I understand that, Riley. Trying to find your way home is... well you're not the only one who's felt that way."

"Yeah, well. About three months after Dad's passing, I woke up one night and Danny was there. He had a knife. And a paper. The paper was a legal form signing the house and all its contents, as well as all the bank accounts, over to him."

"Did he hurt you?" Russell asked, taking mental inventory of his lover's skin. He could recall no suspicious scars.

"No," she replied. "He didn't have to. Seeing him scared me enough… I signed the paper on the spot." She buried her face in his shoulder. "See, I'm a coward."

Russell laid a hand on the center of her back. "You were scared. After what I saw in your dream, it's no wonder. Did he abuse you your whole childhood?"

She shook her head side to side. "It was bad when I was little. When Mom lived with us. She… she was usually not there."

"She left you alone together?" he demanded.

Riley met his eyes, her lip wedged between her teeth. "No. Physically she was present, but mentally… she daydreamed a lot. Humming, but not to me. Did your mother sing to you, Russ?"

"My mother died when I was a cub. I barely remember her. But she didn't sing that I'm aware of."

"Oh." She blinked. "Well mine was always humming, a wordless little tune I've never run into anywhere else. I… I think she made it up. Anyway, she didn't always seem to realize I was there. I could talk right to her, and she wouldn't answer. I learned to fend for myself when I was very small, getting food out of the refrigerator. I would climb up on the sink for a drink of water. If she knew about Danny… well she never seemed to notice it."

Riley's arms snaked around Russell's neck. Sensing she needed a lot of comforting, he cradled her in a loving embrace. His lips brushed her forehead.

"Where did she go, Riley?" he asked.

"I don't know," she replied. "I was about eight. One day she was there, and the next… gone. My father said she had left and wouldn't be back, but he wouldn't say more than that. He never did."

"That's sad," Russ replied.

Riley shrugged. "Much as I hate to say it, things got better after that, for me at least. My father was home more, which I loved. He paid attention to me. He also hired an au pair to watch over me. With her around, Danny didn't corner me nearly as often. I stuck to her like glue. I'm pretty sure she's the one who told my father what Danny was doing. I was sad when she got married and moved to Seattle."

"I bet," Russell said. "Well I'm glad someone looked out for you, Riley."

"Me too." Her face brightened. "A few years before Emma moved, Danny was sent to prison. He got in a bar fight and cut someone up with a knife. They called it attempted homicide. Sad for that guy, but good for me. I was able to finish school, get my teacher certification and teach for two years in safety. Dad's and my relationship was so strong then. I was blessed to have him."

"Sounds like it. I wish I could have met him."

"Me too. He would have liked you, Russ."

Russell wasn't so sure about that, but he didn't say so. Even a gentle soul might have an opinion about a bear hanging around his daughter.

"So, I suppose," he said, changing the subject, "that since you knew Danny wasn't afraid to use a knife on someone..."

"It seemed wisest to give him what he wanted and get the hell out of town," Riley finished for him. "It was hard to leave the house, let me tell you."

"I bet. Poor Riley. No wonder you looked so haunted when you first got to town."

"Do I still look that way?"

He studied her and shook his head. "You look happy." He kissed the end of her nose. "And I'm arrogant enough to take credit for it."

Riley laughed. "Silly man. You don't have to take credit. I was about to give it to you."

He smudged his lips over hers as his stomach let out a ferocious growl. "Come on. Let's get some food before I perish. After so much exertion over the last few days, I need fuel."

"Sounds good. Shall we?"

Russell tucked Riley into her jacket before pulling on his own. A few moments later, clad in scarves, boots and mittens, they ventured into the icy street. The wind stole his breath for a moment, teasing him as it nipped his exposed skin. Riley shivered through all her layers. Luckily, this time their walk only consisted of a few blocks.

The low, red-brick structure of the café stood out like a beacon in the twilight, drawing them into the cozy embrace of its interior. Inside, wood paneling barely peeped out between neon and tin signs advertising everything from beer to motor oil. A football game on the television over the bar had drawn a crowd, one of whom was the school's principal.

"Russ," Bill shouted over the din. Leaving the bar, he approached the couple. "How did you two weather the storm?" He glanced at Riley, who was unwrapping her scarf from around her neck. At the sight of her scarlet blush, he quickly amended, "Scratch that. Glad you two got through safely. Russ, your plane was retrieved Friday. Now that it's had a tree-ectomy and a new windshield installed, it should be good as new."

"Thank you," Russ replied. "I appreciate that."

"No problem. You ready to hit it again tomorrow, Miss Jenkins?"

"Yes, sir," Riley replied. "I'm ready. Looking forward to it."

"Good girl." A loud cheer from the vicinity of the bar drew the principal's gaze. "Damn. Missed a touchdown."

"Go enjoy the game," Russ replied. "We're here to eat anyway."

"Okay. Later." He wandered off.

Russell hung Riley's outerwear on an overburdened coat rack near the door before escorting her to a table, his arm around her waist, keeping her plastered to his side. Heads turned, and eyes stared. Riley's face darkened to nearly purple.

"What are you doing?" she hissed as they slid into a booth. "Were you showing me off or what?"

"Yep," Russ replied unrepentantly.

"Is that really necessary?"

"It is. Sorry if you're uncomfortable, Riley, but you're mine and I need people to know that. It's in my nature. Are you embarrassed to be with me?"

She closed her eyes. "Of course not."

He reached across the table and clasped her hand. "Then what's the big deal? People will find out sooner or later."

"I know," she replied. "I just don't like all the staring."

"I understand. But try not to be upset. This," He lifted their joined hands and kissed her knuckle, "will only be news for a short time. Everyone expected it."

Riley sighed, still looking uncomfortable.

"Something to drink?" Barbara asked, sauntering up, pencil poised over her notepad.

"Coffee, please," Russ requested. "It's damned cold outside."

"It's Alaska," Barbara replied tartly. "You want warmth, try Hawaii. Riley?"

"Hot chocolate sounds good," Riley said.

"I'll be right back with those." Barbara tossed her hair. "Here are some menus, lovebirds. I'll be back in a few."

"I think I'll go into seclusion," Riley said gloomily.

Russell laughed.

* * *

The polar bear lumbered through the snow, snorting and making quiet moaning noises. Loneliness seemed to hold him in a grip more frozen than the icy crust beneath his feet. Throughout decades in near isolation, he'd never felt lonely. Not until this moment. This moment when Riley, his Riley, his mate, slept in her undersize apartment in town while he prowled the edges of his property fifteen miles away. He missed her. The pain felt as though something had been cut away, and yet he was aware how foolishly he was overreacting. *She* is *only fifteen miles away. You can call her tomorrow, or even go see her. You'll see her on Tuesday night.*

The quality of the darkness changed from deepest night to pre-dawn. *You'll have a hell of a day if you don't go to bed, Russ. Why stay up all night?* The voice of reason pleaded with him, but his restless bear wouldn't be calmed. The animal wanted its mate. Wanted her snuggled beside him in the bed and knew the futility of trying to sleep without her.

Stretching up on his hind legs, Russell shredded the bark of his favorite tree with enormous claws. *I hope she decides to move in soon... or I might just camp outside her apartment.*

Chapter 7

By Tuesday, Russell was about to lose his mind. Fatigue from two sleepless nights taxed even the bear's ability to cope, and the tepid, partial satisfaction he received from phone calls did not begin to assuage his longing for his girl. He waited half an hour outside the Golden school complex watching parents collect their little ones. The sight tightened his heart as he considered, for the first time in his life, what it would be like to pick up his own offspring from a school. His and Riley's. He felt a profound gratitude that his mate was a woman of such character. Yes, she was fragile and fearful, but she had the kindest heart.

At last the children were gone and the teachers began to head for the parking lot. Lost in romantic daydreams, he almost missed Riley's arrival. Only the crunch of snow in front of him drew his attention to the petite, caramel-haired woman in front of him.

"Hi," she said shyly, her eyes skating away.

"Hi," he replied. Apparently his tongue had been rendered numb by the impact of her appearance. *Was she always this beautiful? How can I be this hard hit by a woman I've slept with already?* Not caring who might be watching, he laced his fingers into her hair and held her face immobile while he ravaged her mouth with a hot, wild kiss.

"I missed you," she mumbled against his lips.

"Oh, Riley," he rumbled, man and bear voicing the same sentiment, "missed doesn't even come close. Please..." He trailed off, unable to resist kissing her again. And again. And then again. Riley moaned and slipped her arms around his neck, tangling her tongue with his in shameless passion.

A honking horn broke the lovers apart. "Get a room," a male voice hollered. *What a good idea.*

"Riley," he murmured, "let's go back to your place. I need you right now."

"Okay," she agreed.

"I love you," he said. Then he took her hand. The two of them raced through the town back to Riley's apartment. The moment the door clicked shut, jackets flew and then Russell had Riley pressed up against the wall. "Don't make me sleep alone again," he urged.

"No, of course not," she replied. "This was hell."

"I'll get you wherever you need to be, but you have to stay with me."

"I will," she vowed.

"No more sleeping in studios." He unzipped her pants and tugged them down her thighs.

"No, nor spare bedrooms. I can't stand it, Russ." She yanked his shirt over his head.

"I know what you mean." Russell dropped to his knees. The scent of Riley's overwhelming arousal teased his senses. Leaving the wall to support her weight, he hooked one of her legs over his shoulder and leaned forward.

"Russell?" she whimpered.

He spread her folds and indulged in a long perusal of her swollen, glistening womanhood. With his middle and ring fingers, he spread her honey over every inch. The tiny opening of her body tempted him even as the desire to claim her overwhelmed him. He slipped his middle finger into her. A quiet whine escaped and she clamped down on his fingers. The tightness teased him. He couldn't wait to stretch that tiny vessel open with his aching heat. Unable to resist, he added his ring finger. Riley's whimper turned to a yelp.

"Did I hurt you?" he asked.

"Noooo." Her answer blended into a pleasured cry. Reassured, he gently began to ease his fingers in and out, preparing her for intercourse while he leaned forward. Her clitoris stood dark and swollen, begging for his attention. He tongued the eager nub. Riley cried out. Russell wanted to taste her orgasm before he filled her. Riley arched her hips, pressing herself closer to him. He grinned. She wanted his touch. Her salty-sweet honey tingled on his tongue, electrifying his arousal. He lapped at her, enjoying her eager, uninhibited response, driving her recklessly into pleasure.

"Russ... oh God!" Riley rocked her hips, one moment pressing close, the next drawing away. He followed her lead, knowing how intense this kind of loving could be. Rolling his eyes upward, he was able to see her, her fingers digging into the fabric of the sweater she hadn't managed to pull off in their rush. Her whole sex was clenching and fluttering as ecstasy neared.

"Russell..." She drew his name out long.

"I've got you," he said. "Fly, Riley."

Her head thumped against the wall as wails of pleasure seemed to be ripped from her throat.

"That's my girl." He eased her gently through her moment of bliss, then slowly lowered her down, supporting her limp, pleasure-drained body until her two feet rested on the floor and drawing off what was left of her clothing until she stood bare before him.

He kept his eyes on Riley's lovely face and naked, ready body as he stripped off his own boots, jeans, boxers and socks. She watched through half-lidded eyes.

"Ready, love?"

"Oh yes." A new spark flared in her languid eyes and she straightened, grasping his offered hand and allowing him to lead her to her bed. This time it had been folded up into a sofa. Russell sat and urged Riley onto his lap, but she resisted.

"What is it?"

Her cheeks pinkened, but she dropped to her knees before him. "My turn."

"Riley, you don't need to do that!" But even as he spoke, Russ' erection jumped in eager anticipation.

"I want to." This time she leaned into him and kissed the tip of his penis. He groaned and pushed his fingers into her hair.

She kissed him again, this time letting the tip of her tongue slip between her lips so she could taste the drop of pre-ejaculate that had gathered at his opening.

"Hmmm." She looked up at him and smiled.

"Good?" he asked.

"I like it." Parting her lips, Riley took the head of Russell's sex in her mouth, teasing all the way around with curious licks.

Russell had had many blow jobs in his life, but nothing could compare with the sweet innocence of Riley's mouth. She was pure passion, giving generously because it was what she wanted. Because his pleasure meant that much to her. Her desire to please him felt so strong, Russ could almost smell it. *So this is love. I thought I knew, but I had no idea. Give and take. Try to give more.*

Then thought shattered as Riley's mouth slipped further down on his erection. She knew enough to imitate what he would soon be doing to her, sliding up and down on his sex as she held him in place with one hand. Her tongue lashed sweetly over his heated flesh until he ached for release. *But not like this. I need to be inside my girl.* "Riley..."

She released him with a pop and lifted her head.

"Come here, sweet girl. I need you."

Biting her lip, she took his hand and straddled his lap. Her eyes skated away from his, even as his fingers delved between her folds, seeking her most sensitive spot and stroking it.

"Shy, Riley? Why? We've had sex before."

She swallowed hard. "I don't know. It feels... more momentous. Like we're sealing some kind of vow." She wrapped her fingers around his shaft.

"Maybe we are." His free hand went to her hip, urging her closer to him. "Is that a problem?"

Riley moved into position over Russell's waiting penis. She held him as he pressed down on her flank, and he sank slowly into wet, silken depths that gripped him with delicious tightness.

"Did you really mean it?" she asked breathlessly as she began to rise and fall on him. He never broke rhythm with his stimulation of her clitoris. "Do you really love me? I mean… it's so soon."

"Riley…" Russell had to grit out the words between clenched teeth. "Riley, you know it works differently for me." He groaned. *God, that's good.* "Or does it? Do you really not feel it too?"

"I feel something." She panted. "I don't know…"

"You do," he replied. "I know you do. Don't be afraid, Riley. Trust me."

"I… Oooooh!" Ecstasy overwhelmed her and she shuddered. The luscious clenching of her sweet sex brought Russell right to the brink of his own orgasm. Holding her tight in both hands, he began to thrust hard into her yielding body. This intense stimulation, it seemed, kept her locked in her peak until he could join her there. Russell roared as pleasure slammed him with an almost painful force.

He emerged slowly to find Riley's fingertips over his mouth. Setting her back a bit, he stared at her.

"You were making bear noises. I didn't want the neighbors to call animal control," she explained.

"We can't do this here," he replied. *Good Lord.*

"It's okay, Russell. We don't have to. I decided yesterday I wanted to move in with you."

"You didn't say anything on the phone," he pointed out.

"It seemed better to say it in person."

Unable to argue with her logic, he settled her bare body back against his. She rested her head on his shoulder. He traced one thumb up and down her spine.

Long moments passed as they cuddled in languid contentment, her body soft and warm against his. Outside the window, twilight shadows grew and lengthened. At last, Riley sighed and rose from his lap.

He helped her to her feet. Riley grimaced and hurried to the bathroom. *Oops. Spontaneous sex and no towel.* Then he realized what they'd done – what they'd been doing – and grimaced. Snow-bound together, aroused and trapped, nature had taken its course, but it had not been planned, and he hadn't had what he needed.

Riley emerged from the bathroom a moment later, wearing blue and white boy shorts. With her breasts bare, she cut quite a compelling figure. Russell couldn't stop himself from taking a taste of each perky nipple.

"Cut that out," Riley protested. "If you start that again, we'll never get home. You'll end up stuck here in this little apartment until tomorrow."

Russell looked down at his muscular body. "I don't think I'll fit," he commented. "So get dressed."

She gave him a questioning look.

"What, honey?"

"How do we do this?"

"I have a suggestion," he replied. "What do you say about this...? Call Lakeville. Let them know I'll bring you in the morning."

She bit her lip. "That's a good idea. Okay."

"And in the meanwhile, get dressed. My place is bigger. Let's go."

As she started tugging on her clothes, he added, "You know, I just realized something."

"What's that?" Riley clipped her bra behind her back and reached for her jeans.

"We… um we haven't been using protection."

"Oh." Riley paused, her turtleneck over her head, but her arms not in the sleeves. "Is that a bad thing, Russ? Do you have a dangerous disease I should know about? I mean, my sexual history – or lack thereof – was pretty obvious. But you, being skilled and older, must have some experience."

Russ sighed. "Yeah. It's tradition among the bears that when a male reaches sexual maturity, about at age 25, one of the older women initiates him. I had an experience like that. And… well it's been a lot of years since then. I've had a few partners. Mostly bear shifters, and they don't get diseases. I won't get you sick, Riley. But what about pregnancy? Shifters are less prolific than humans, but it's still a possibility."

Finally dressed, Riley stepped close to Russ and looped her arms around his neck, captivating him with her intoxicating eyes. "Russell, what do I do for a living?"

"You teach," he replied, wondering where this was headed.

"I teach *kindergarten*," she reminded him. "I teach little, tiny kids. Guess why?"

"You like kids?" he suggested.

"Bingo. I like kids. I want kids. The way you talk about us, about fate and mates and commitments, if I should happen to conceive, you'll still be there, right?"

"Of course!" The image of Riley, her belly heavily pushed out with his child, tightened his breath.

"Do you want children?" she asked, her face twisting in a wistful expression.

"I do," he replied. "I do very much. Not to mention, there aren't so many shifters around. We'd be on the endangered species list, if anyone knew we existed. Reproducing is expected of all mated couples."

"There," she said. "I think we're okay then."

"Riley, you blow me away," he said.

Her mouth quirked in a half smile. "Um, I would have a baby, and not a cub, right? I mean, that's not much to ask."

"I have no control over the form our children would take, honey," he informed her. "It seems likely we'd have human babies, though probably with extra abilities. But I'm half human and you're fully human, so the odds are in your favor."

"Russell," she mumbled into his skin.

"Hmmmm?"

"I… I do love you."

A slow smile curved his lips upward. "I'm glad. I think everything will be okay now."

"I know it will."

Not expecting such a definite statement, Russell touched his lips to Riley's temple. "How do you know?"

"Because I do trust you."

He hugged her. *Is it really going to be this easy?* He hoped so because right in that moment, life seemed damned near perfect.

Chapter 8

That night, she lay beside him in the bed they now shared, studying the wood grain of the exposed beams in the ceiling, and pondering it. *I didn't come to Alaska to find love, but to find safety and a new beginning.* Russell let out a rumbling snore, his warm breath moistening the back of her neck. One big hand cupped her breast and his sex, now relaxed from recent loving and sleep, pressed against her bottom. From the bed, she could see the window. The blinds stood open because after all, they only had one neighbor, and her house was on the other side. Only moose and deer might peek in at them. Even bears hesitated to tangle with the strange-smelling near-bear they knew lived inside. Riley snuggled back against Russell. His warmth made her feel amazing. Safe in a way she hadn't known existed. *He's so nothing like I imagined.* Even with her back to him, she could see the shiny white of his hair, his deeply bronzed skin. The sexy creases around his eyes and mouth. Mature men were hot in a way words couldn't even describe, and she'd never realized it. *Not until I set eyes on Russell that first time. It was like… learning to breathe. I wonder if he's right about fate and complimentary DNA. It would explain why I feel… so perfectly matched with him. Why everything he suggests is something I already want. I like this, but it's confusing.* Or at least, Riley felt confused when she stopped to analyze their relationship rationally. When she just let it be, she felt perfectly at peace.

Even his snores are soothing. She laughed to herself. What a radical change to go from shy, frightened mouse to confident, sexually active woman in just a few short months. *I didn't expect to like sex quite so much either.* Now, it appeared, Riley was completely addicted not only to Russell's company, but also to those special moments when their bodies merged. *He knows what he's doing. All those decades of experience, and he plays my body like a musical instrument.* She tingled with the memory. *I love this. The sun may not rise for the next month, but being able to wake up in Russell's arms, and spend my first wakeful moments face down in the mattress while he...* Even the image of him 'mating' her, as he liked to call it when he took her from behind, heated her face and body. Though already drenched from their just-completed sex, fresh moisture surged between her thighs. Russell rumbled in his sleep, his hand releasing her breast and sliding down her belly to tease her mound. She drew in an unsteady breath. *Greedy girl. You just had sex. Do you really need more?* her conscience scolded, even as she drew one knee up to allow Russell's sleepy questing. She wanted to purr. Even this light touch stimulated her overwrought nerve endings and drew a quiet whimper from her throat. Then Russell sighed in his sleep and rolled over. His soft snoring resumed. Riley couldn't help laughing at herself. *Tomorrow, Riley. Go to sleep. You'll have plenty of opportunities tomorrow.*

* * *

A cozy night, in the annoying way all perfect moments have, passed far too quickly. Before she knew it, Russell was flying her over hills and forests back to Lakeville for her Wednesday with the eight local munchkins. Though she felt more than a fleeting pang over being separated from Russell, who had become something dangerously close to her reason for breathing, she felt energized from her decision to move in with him, relaxed and ready to tackle the day. Story books and letter charts awaited her in the classroom, ready to be put to use, and she had on sturdy winter outwear – and underwear – for her turn as playground monitor. But best of all, two hours after the students went home, Russ would be collecting her and taking her back to his place… *our place…* for the night. A slow smile spread across Riley's lips as the little plane bumped to a stop on the makeshift runway. She'd be having early mornings on Wednesdays and Thursdays, because Russ refused to let her sleep another night with Carrolls. She didn't mind.

"What's got you so smiley, sweet girl?" he asked in that sexy, low-pitched rumble of his as the plane shuddered and the engine stilled.

"Oh, nothing," she replied, flirtatiously twining her hair around one finger. "I'm just really happy is all."

It seemed he heard the message she hadn't voiced, because he grasped her hand in his and kissed her fingertips, his face lighting up. *It amazes me I can have such an effect on him. I've been practically invisible most of my life, and now I have this sexy older man acting like I'm his sunshine.* Russell slid his fingers up her arm and laced them into the back of her hair. Riley knew what that meant and leaned forward at his urging, accepting his kiss. *I love you, Russell,* she thought as hard as she could. *I can't explain or even understand how this happened so quickly, but I can't deny the reality. I love you.*

He heard the thought and responded by coiling his tongue around hers. She broke away with a gasp. "Don't be evil. If I have to spend the day all wet and achy, the kids are going to suffer."

Russell pouted, poking out his lower lip in a silly parody of disappointment. "I'll miss you all day."

She softened her mock outrage. "I know. I'll miss you too. But, honey, I live with you now.

We can make love all night and weekend, every night and weekend until we're sick of it."

"Riley." Russell's rumble had lowered to nearly a growl. "Do you honestly think I'll ever get sick of you? Because that won't happen."

Tears sprang to her eyes and her throat clogged, but she fought down her emotions. *Don't start the day off crying. It's too draining.*

"Say it," he urged.

"I love you."

The chiseled planes of his left cheek lifted into a half-smile and he nodded.

"I love you too, Riley. Now go teach the munchkins. I'll be back at five to take you home."

She tugged him over for one more kiss and then jumped down from the plane, hurrying through the biting early-morning cold to set up her classroom for the day.

In truth, Riley did struggle to pay attention to her job throughout the day. It took all her willpower to push Russell out of her mind and focus on the eight small people she was supposed to be teaching, but in the end, the kindergartners won. The moment her mind wandered, pandemonium broke out, in the form of a paint fight.

Sighing, she cleaned up the messy kids, thankful as always that she'd paid extra for the washable paints, and set the perpetrator in the 'thinking chair' for ten minutes. After that, she'd forced herself to stay fully present with the class.

At last they marched down the hall to the music room and Riley took the opportunity to walk the twenty steps down the street to the Carrolls' house.

Mrs. Carroll, a middle-aged woman with silver wings in her dark hair and high cheekbones that contrasted strikingly with bright blue eyes, ushered her into a familiar family room whose cheerfully clashing décor spoke of a multigenerational family home. Sleek leather sectionals paired with glass end tables made little sense placed alongside a rustic wooden hutch cluttered with far too many tchotchkes. Riley couldn't help smiling at the sight. It reminded her of her father's home, though he collected books, books and more books, not carved wooden animals and teacups in fussy patterns.

"What can I do for you today, Riley?" Mrs. Carroll asked. "Can I get you anything?"

"I can only stay a minute," Riley replied. "The kids will be done in music before you know it, but I needed to let you know..." Her face heated and she had to take a deep breath before she could continue. "I met someone and... and he asked me to move in with him, so I won't need to sleep here anymore. I really appreciate your hospitality though."

Mrs. Carroll's face twisted into a concerned expression. "That's pretty fast, Riley."

"I know." The warmth in her cheeks turned to a burning sensation. "But sometimes you just *know*, you know?" Internally she rolled her eyes at her ineloquent comment.

"That doesn't make me feel any better, Riley. Are you sure this is a good idea?" Mrs. Carroll laid a hand on her arm.

Riley nodded. "I know it seems... maybe not so wise, but I just feel like Russ... well he's worth the risk."

The older woman's eyes widened. "Russ Tadzea?"

At Riley's next nod, she visibly relaxed. "Oh, wow. I've never known Russ to do anything like this. But he's a good, steady, reliable man. You'll be fine with him, Riley. Congratulations."

Riley grinned. Russ had a powerful impact on everyone.

"He's a werewolf," a cracked and wavering voice emerged from the corner. Riley turned and as expected, Grandmother Carroll was waving a gnarled and bony finger in her direction. The woman's hair seemed to vibrate in her agitation, the tight, white perm trembling around her brown face like a dandelion seed in the wind.

Riley approached the elderly woman and took her hand. "I promise you, Mrs. Carroll, Russ is no werewolf."

"He is," the old woman repeated stubbornly, "and you're a floozy."

"Well, I'm a happy floozy." Stung, Riley moved away from the old woman. "I need to get back to class. See you later, Mrs. Carroll."

"Riley..." The younger woman began, casting a glare at her mother-in-law.

"It's okay. I have to go, though." Riley said. "And I really do appreciate you letting me stay with you these last couple of months."

Without another word, Riley moved through the door and hiked down the freezing street back into the school building, glad she didn't leave things there when she was away, but just kept a packed overnight bag. *Great. Now I'm going to have to try even harder to concentrate.*

* * *

By the time 5pm rolled around, Riley had developed a massive headache. Apart from the normal kindergarten stresses of hair pulling, potty accidents and broken crayons, the unpleasantness of Grandmother Carroll's unfounded accusations bit at her. *Werewolves are one thing, but a floozy? I've had sex with one man in my life.* She rolled her eyes, telling herself furiously, once again, to let it go. *She's an old woman with a sour disposition. She's probably bored, so she picks at people to pass the time. It's not personal. She barely knows you. Even staying there you didn't exchange more than about ten words a day.* Sighing, she moved through her classroom, righting an overturned chair here, straightening a poster there. She wondered for the first time about the wisdom of what she was doing. Yes, there was something special about Russell, and she felt tremendously drawn to him, but could she truly trust him? "And why not?" she asked herself aloud. "When has he ever done anything untrustworthy?" *There's a lot he still hasn't told you.* "Of course. He has to let things out little by little, but that doesn't mean he's hiding them. He's only waiting for the right time. I love Russell." *Love what he does to you in bed,* the sly little voice teased. *Maybe you really are a floozy.* "Stop it, Riley," she told herself insistently. "I sleep with him because I love him and want to be close to him. It's a normal thing to do."

"This sounds intense."

Riley squeaked in surprised as warm arms enfolded her from behind. Then her face flamed, realizing she'd been caught talking to herself.

"Sorry," she mumbled.

"Hey, no worries," he replied. "It's a big transition. I'm not surprised you have a few doubts. I'm just thankful you're willing to face them with me."

She turned and laid one hand on the back of his neck, stroking the silky white hairs there. "Of course." A little tug had his lips in prime kissing position and she wasted no time claiming them. Here, in his arms, bathed in his scent, everything made sense again.

"Ready to go?" he asked, stepping back and taking her hand.

"Almost. I'm not quite dressed to go outside yet."

In her hurry to get home, pulling on her outerwear seemed to take forever. As Riley pulled off her flats and replaced them with snow boots, Russell said, "Did something happen?"

"I ran into Grandmother Carroll," Riley replied. She shoved her shoes in her satchel and reached for her coat.

"Sorry." Russell winced and helped her pull up the zipper.

"I'm surprised, in the Twenty-First Century," Riley continued as she settled her knitted cap on her head and began shoving her hands into fat and puffy gloves, "that a couple living together would cause anyone to raise an eyebrow. I thought you said people were open-minded here."

Russell moved faster than she would have thought possible, especially given his size. Between one breath and the next he had her face in his hand and was kissing her again, a brief, wet smooch. "Most people are. But keep in mind that Grandmother Carroll is old and cranky. Her issues are her own. You don't have to make them yours."

"I know," Riley replied. "I keep telling myself that."

"Well, don't stop. I love you and I want you with me every minute. That isn't going to change. Not for one grouchy old lady, that's for sure. I hope you feel the same way."

"Of course I do, Russ," Riley assured him. "I'm not leaving because werewolf-woman has an issue. I just didn't like being called a floozy. I'll be better tomorrow."

Russell turned one corner of his mouth upward in a grim parody of a smile. "I feel sorry for Mrs. Carroll. Imagine living with that woman and her nasty comments full time."

"You know," Riley said as they turned and headed toward the door, "I was thinking exactly the same thing."

"Besides, she's wrong. You're a good girl who loves her man. It's only natural."

Riley smiled. "You'd know better than most." Outside, a frigid wind blasted her in the face, stealing her breath. She gasped.

Russ laughed. "You'll get used to it."

Riley glared evilly at him and struggled to draw air into her lungs as they crossed the parking lot and rounded the fence to the air strip, where his tiny plane waited to take them home. *Home.* Despite her rough day, the thought of the cabin filled her with a warm glow and set anticipation simmering in her belly. The heat in Russell's black eyes told her what they'd be doing when they got there. *Eat your heart out, old woman. I'll be busy loving my man and not caring what you think.*

Once he had the plane in the air, Russell spoke again. "I have to go away for a few days, Riley."

She blinked. "Why? What's up?" She glanced at her beloved and noticed that his expression had turned grim.

"One of my uncles died. They're having a Potlatch for him this weekend. I've already requested a couple of personal days to attend it.

I'm only staying Friday through Monday and I'll be home Tuesday, so you won't need to worry about the plane. Just take the snowmobile to Golden on Monday."

Riley pondered in silence. The thought of Russell leaving didn't feel right. She wasn't settled enough in his cabin to want to be there without him. Nor did several nights' separation sit well with her, but her swirling thoughts refused to coalesce, so she asked a different question. "I've heard the term 'Potlatch' before. Isn't it a kind of party?"

He nodded. "Yeah. We dance, chant, and eat. Gifts are given. That sort of thing."

His terse response begged more questions, but Riley wasn't quite sure how to ask them. Russell seemed distant, his eyes scanning the horizon.

"I'm sorry about your uncle," she said at last.

"It's all right, Riley. He was very old, and his health had long since failed. He was ready. This Potlatch will be a celebration of his life."

"I like that idea," she said. "Were... were you very close to him?"

His eyes slanted sideways at her for a brief moment before returning to the fast-approaching hills. Without the icy sleet to slow the plane, he was able to crest them easily. The treetops clustering the summit seemed to reach like tickling fingers for the belly of the plane, quivering in a slow wind. "Not really. I grew up with my mother's family. Her brother, for the most part."

"Interesting." Riley didn't know what to make of that.

"It's fairly traditional in both the Native and Bear clans. The mother's brother features heavily in bringing up children, teaching them the ways of their people. Because I can shift, I was kept with the bears when I was weaned, whereas my brother, who does not have that ability, went to our father and has been trained to lead the community after Father passes."

Though the information fascinated Riley, the tense set of Russell's jaw in no way resembled the relaxed manner in which he'd regaled her with other werebear tales. Apparently, while his culture was dear to him, his own experiences caused some pain.

"Will I ever get to meet them?" she asked.

This time he turned his entire head and looked at her in consternation. "Meet my family?"

"Yes, Russell," she said, enunciating slowly, just shy of sarcasm. "Isn't meeting family members part of being in a relationship?"

He blinked, shook his head and returned his attention to flying the plane. "Yes, I suppose so. I mean, you can meet my dad's family. That would be okay. I'll contact him, ask if you can come to the Potlatch."

"And your mother's family? You said your mother died, right?"

"Yes, when I was a small cub. I was raised by my uncle, like I told you, but I can't take you there. It's too dangerous."

His eyes slid her direction, took in her questioning stare and elaborated.

"The shifters are a secretive lot. They'd prefer if only our brother tribe knew they existed, and even they are not allowed to know where the village is. Far as I know, I'm the only one who knows where they live but who is not part of the community. They barely tolerate me. If we went together, they'd kill us both."

"Russ..."

He sighed. "I know, I know. Time to come clean, right? Yes, I grew up there. Now I'm not welcome to live with them anymore because of something that happened when I started puberty. Okay, are you ready for another story, this one absolutely true and not lore?"

Riley tugged off her glove and laid her hand on Russell's. "I want to hear everything about you."

He grinned, but the lack of humor transformed his expression to a grimace.

Alarmed, a thousand random and pointless thoughts raged through Riley's head, crowding one over another so tight and close that not one could squirm free and force itself between her lips.

"Slow down your racing mind, Riley," Russ said wryly. "I'm not a criminal or anything. It's not something I had control over. Okay, listen, honey. Let me explain a little bit about what it means to be what I am."

At her nod, he continued.

"A bear shifter mother only has one cub at a time. Even twins are almost unheard of. That doesn't change when she's mated with a human. The only thing that can be affected is whether the offspring is a cub, who will learn to change shapes at puberty, or a human."

His eyes met hers and she dipped her chin again, showing she was paying attention.

"When the baby is weaned, about at age two, the humans are taken to their fathers in the Den'a village, which is what happened to my younger brother. The cubs stay with the mother's brother, which is why I was raised by my uncle…"

"So whether Native or shifter," Riley interrupted, "no mother gets to keep her baby after the age of two?" The very thought made her insides jump.

"That's right," he replied.

"Well, if you think I'm going to hand over our baby, you're crazy."

He turned his head fully away from the horizon to stare at her. "Are you…"

"Watch out." Riley pointed at a fast-approaching tree. Russell jerked the plane upward with a nauseating jolt. "I don't know yet," she added. "But you can't deny it's a possibility. We've done nothing to prevent it."

He sighed. "I know."

"And it's not a problem," she said. "I like kids, remember?"

This time the smile that curved his lips looked genuine. "So do I. Don't worry, Riley. I realize you aren't a part of either of those cultures. Realistically, neither am I anymore. Any babies we have will stay with us until they're grown, I promise. I wouldn't ask anything else of you."

"Good," Riley said. "Now, I believe you were explaining to me why you're no longer part of either culture?"

His grin disappeared. *Wow. This must be really hard for him.* Riley reached over and laid a hand on Russell's, stroking the skin on the backs of his fingers.

"Yeah, well. I'm a freak, or so they say. I shouldn't exist."

Riley's eyebrows drew together as confusion churned.

"See, shape-shifters don't have psychic abilities. They can change shapes, detect scents. Anything a bear can do, a shifter can do, but not sending and receiving thoughts. That's inherited from my father's side. It's a human ability. Up to this point, there was no crossover between the abilities. Shifters aren't psychic and psychics don't shift. When I reached puberty and began sending thoughts to the other bears, they realized I wasn't normal and sent me to my father. But it created a conundrum, because I didn't have control over my shifting abilities either. One minute, I'd look like a youth, the next like a polar bear. It freaked people out. So the bears don't want me because I'm psychic, but the humans don't want me because I'm a bear. I'm screwed. Didn't you ever wonder why I would chose to live among white people? It wasn't for the money, I promise you."

Riley blinked. "That's pretty sad."

"You're telling me," Russell replied. "I didn't like being cast out of the Winter River shifter community. Especially not when the Den'a village was no more welcoming."

"I'm sorry, honey," Riley said, her stroking fingers taking in his whole hand.

"It's long in the past," he replied. "They both tolerate me – barely. And I have a good job I love and now…" He lifted her hand to his lips. "Now I also have a beautiful mate I love. So really, life isn't bad."

"Hurry home," Riley urged. *He'll never admit how much it still bothers him, but I want to make it better.*

His tongue snaked out and teased the tender skin between her knuckles. She shivered.

The remaining fifteen minutes of the flight seemed to last fifteen hours. By the time the plane bumped to a stop in Golden and Russell helped Riley to the ground, she was nearly quivering with anticipation, and they still had a long snowmobile ride ahead of them. Grinding her teeth, she dragged Russell around the back of the district's transportation building: a shed large enough to house the tiny plane and one single school bus. Out back, Russell's snowmobile had been chained to a tree.

He chuckled as she tapped her foot impatiently, twirling the lock with slow deliberation that made her want to scream.

"Glad to hear you're feeling happier," she snapped.

"My girl is in a hurry to make love. Why would I not be happy?" he teased.

"Stop it," Riley hissed, clapping her gloves onto cheeks that should have been much, much colder. The touch of icy leather on her skin only intensified the burn. "Someone might hear."

"Riley, honey," he said as he rolled up the chain and tucked it into the compartment under the seat, "we live together. People have already guessed we're sleeping together. Are you really that embarrassed?"

Riley made a face. "Not really, I guess. I just feel like... I feel like it should be private."

He caught her chin in one hand and kissed her lips. "Okay, shy baby. We'll be a picture of discretion... in public. But once I get you home... watch out."

"Sounds perfect," Riley agreed, wrinkling her nose.

"Climb on, Riley-girl," Russ urged. "Let's get home where we can be indiscreet in private."

Riley straddled the snowmobile and Russell fired the engine, roaring down the snowy street and out of town. She cuddled against his back, imagining she could feel his body heat through all the layers of their clothing. "I love you," she murmured into his jacket, even though she knew he couldn't hear, even with his powerful ursine hearing. Long as the flight had taken, the ride took even longer. Riley, still adjusting to her relationship, hungered to be as close to Russell as possible.

At least now, huddled against his back, they were touching.

About five lifetimes later, they pulled to a halt in front of the cabin. Riley had adjusted to riding on the snowmobile and no longer ached and wobbled when she climbed off. Fishing the keys out of his pocket, she hurried to unlock the cabin door while he parked the snowmobile in the shed.

The inside of their home was cold and dark after spending the day standing empty, and Riley turned on all the lights in the great room before approaching the fireplace. Contemplating the empty grate, she wondered if she'd learned enough from watching Russ do this to manage it herself. Then, not wanting to burn the house down, she gave up and turned to the thermostat, setting the central heating to a more comfortable temperature. The machine came to life with a whooshing hum and a blast of moving air.

By that time, Russell had made his way into the room and took Riley in his arms.

"What would you like for dinner?" he asked.

"You," she replied, tugging him down so she could kiss his lips.

"Hey, wait!" he protested, laughing. "I'm the predator here."

She arched her eyebrow. "Humans eat bears. I'm the apex predator in this room."

Laughing, they stripped off their outerwear, hanging jackets on the coat rack inside the door, leaving their boots on the welcome mat. When Riley removed her hat, she knew her static laden hair had begun to fly in all directions. Russell's snicker confirmed it. Of course, his neatly trimmed white strands stayed exactly in place.

"That's it," she muttered, trying to flatten the runaway strands. "I'm getting a buzz cut."

"Don't you dare," Russell insisted, his bear growling a warning through his human lips.

Riley grinned. Teasing a bear was a synonym for danger, but she felt no fear. Russell, for all that he wasn't quite human, would never harm her. *Most I could incite him to do is love me hard.* She sashayed over to him, working the buttons of her blouse as she went.

“Oh yeah? What are you going to do about it, big boy?” The garment dropped to the floor behind her, leaving her in a sleeveless camisole so sheer it left the lace pattern of her bra visible. Russ growled again, but she had already learned the meanings of his bear noises. Now, mock irritation was giving way to desire. *Just what I wanted.*

She worked the clasp of her pants, cursing the thick long underwear she wore underneath. Though necessary for all outdoor activities during winter, the thermals were far from sexy. She tugged both layers off at once.

Standing before him with bare legs and arms, she reached for the hem of her camisole. He arrested her hand. “Oh no you don’t,” he rumbled. “That’s my job.”

“Hmmm.” The sound Riley emitted had elements of both hum and whimper. Barred from stripping herself any further, she unbuckled Russell’s belt instead. The fastenings of his jeans next succumbed to her nimble fingers. Then the buttons of his red flannel shirt.

“In a hurry, princess?” he asked.

"Don't tease me, Russ. Not today," she urged, pulling his shirt down his arms so it could fall to the floor. A little twitch sent his jeans pooling around his ankles and he stepped free. "Too many layers."

"Easy, girl. We have all night." He lifted her cami over her head and unhooked her bra. "I've missed these," he rumbled, lifting one breast in each hand and leaning down to lick and nip each bright pink nipple. They reacted to his touch and the cold in the room, springing to full engorgement. He clamped down on one, sucking and tugging it.

Riley's knees buckled. Russ sensed it immediately and grasped her hips, easing her onto the bearskin in front of the cold fireplace. Then he stripped off his undershirt and boxers. At the sight of his hugely swollen erection, Riley let out a little coo of pleasure and wrapped her hand around the thick shaft. She wouldn't be satisfied until all that rigid heat was buried to the hilt inside her. Her passage seemed to melt into wet, fiery readiness, moisture gathering on the lips of her sex. Russell eased her panties down her thighs.

"Hmmm," he rumbled, nuzzling into her wetness. "You smell so good when you're turned on. I love that you can't hide your desire. I've been wanting a taste of this since you got into the plane."

Shameless, Riley opened her thighs to admit Russell's probing tongue. He lapped and nibbled at her lacy folds and slipped into her well, but avoided her clitoris.

"Russell," she whined, needing direct stimulation.

He laughed at her eagerness. "Don't rush, sweet girl."

"Please. I need you." She stroked her fingers through his silky white hair.

"How can I resist your begging? All right, Riley. Is this what you need?" He lapped at the swollen center of her pleasure.

Immediately, gasping cries of ecstasy tumbled from Riley's lips. She'd known sex was supposed to feel good, but she'd never imagined the exquisite pleasure Russell's fingers, tongue and penis elicited. She would have feared becoming addicted, but she knew she could trust him. Since addiction was inevitable, Riley succumbed as always. Somehow, resisting Russell never turned out to be what she wanted. Now, as always, she completely gave herself over to his touch. It was as though she ceased to exist as an individual person and merged her entire being into his… into theirs. They were one, not only in the bedroom, but in everything. A new creature forged from all the messy, jumbled, impossible shards that made up their damaged souls. Russell filled in her broken places, and it seemed she filled in his, in a way that neither of them could do alone. That was the thought, though she knew he didn't realize it, that he sent her every time they touched.

As Russell worked her closer to orgasm, Riley's overwhelming desire to draw her lover even closer became impossible to ignore.

"Please," she begged again, reaching for him."

"You're so close, sweet girl." Russ said. "Patience."

"No, I need you now," she forced out, laying her hand on his face. "Russell, now!"

"I want you to come," he protested, running his thumb over her clit.

"I will… once you're inside me."

Russell gave in quickly, to Riley's relief. In another moment his bulky body was pressing her into the bearskin. Nestled between her parted thighs, he sought and found her entrance and slid deep.

Riley's toes curled. The arches of her feet seemed to flutter. Her belly clenched. "Oh!" she half gasped, half moaned. Russell pulled back and pushed in again, and Riley lifted her bottom up to meet his thrust with greedy eagerness.

Cupping the back of his neck in one hand, she drew him down and captured his lips in a loving kiss. Every drive of his sex into her body made shivery bolts of pleasure shoot from the depths of her womanhood up and out, causing her fingers to dig into the rug. The moment gathered taut like a drawn bowstring and Riley lay poised like an arrow, ready to be sprung. Passion, love, desire and trust all flew free at the same instant, in a typhoon of emotion and sensation that crashed over Riley, submerging her completely, so that she was scarcely aware when Russell drove deep and once again bestowed his ecstasy inside her waiting body.

As awareness returned like pinpricks of light in the expanse of midnight heaven, she murmured, "I love you." The light gathered and coalesced into Russell's beautiful dark eyes, which shone down into hers like wild stars.

Chapter 9

Riley clutched tight to Russell's hand as he walked her into the Den'a village. Though always shy when meeting new people, her keen curiosity kept her eyes darting everywhere. Despite frigid sub-zero temperatures, in the heavy hide and fur outfit he'd insisted she wear she felt somewhat less cold than she'd suspected. A small, frozen river cut through the land, and the town, she saw, had been situated around it, a small ring of long, low cabins, the structures formed of spruce logs. The largest, to which Russ was steering her at top speed, not wanting frostbite to reach through her scarf and hurt her, had been cut into a low hillside. *Smart. Use the earth to provide natural temperature regulation.* Three towering totem poles, two with wings, all with brightly colored faces, clustered together, seeming to guard the town with their unearthly presence. They watched her with painted eyes, daring her to cause trouble. *No worries,* she thought. *The last thing I want to do is threaten anyone.*

"In the summer," he informed her, his voice muffled under layers of fabric, "wild flowers grow all around here, and the stream runs with fish. I'll show you some time. But right now…"

"Right now the world is holding its breath," she finished for him. "Waiting for the light and the heat to return."

"Well put, love." His eyes twinkled. "You'll fit in just fine."

Riley wasn't sure about that. After all, if Russell, who had their blood flowing in his veins, was barely tolerated, how was a white girl from the lower 48 supposed to? But she soldiered on, discomfort squirming in her belly. She wanted to meet her boyfriend's people, and she wasn't about to let her own shyness get in her way.

Russell steered her through the doorway into a large, open room. The walls of unplastered round logs blocked the wind and added the warmth of their dark, natural color to the space. Pale partial daylight – the only sort available in deep winter – filtered through small, sparkling clean windows to cast shapes and patterns on the wooden floor and colorful rugs. Furs hung on the walls, as well as narrow fringed blankets in purple and taupe with hints of red. An old man and a middle aged one rose from their seats on a black leather sofa and approached.

"Father, Randy." Riley's eyes slid to Russell, whose voice suddenly sounded less muffled. He'd removed his muffler from his face and lowered his hood. *Good job, Riley, you're standing there like a totem pole. Take off your scarf, doofus.* Tugging the furry hood down from around her face, she unwound the muffler concealing her face.

"Son, welcome," the old man intoned. "Is this the woman you mentioned?"

"Yes, Father," Russell replied. "This is Riley. Riley, my father, Norman Tadzea."

"Welcome," the man said, though his flat inflection did not sound particularly welcoming. Not unwelcoming either, just... flat.

"Thank you for inviting me," she replied. "I want to apologize in advance for any mistakes I make. I'm not familiar with your culture and I don't know how to act."

"I understand," the man said. "We will educate you."

"I appreciate that," she replied.

Then the younger man – Russell's brother, apparently – addressed her. "Don't worry too much, Riley. We've all met white people before. Mostly they come through in large groups in summer, looking for a 'cultural experience'. We tolerate them."

"I'm sure," she replied. "But I don't want to come across as an idle gawker... though I'm sure I will for a while."

"Russell has never brought a woman to meet us before. We will help you," the middle aged man insisted, a gentle smile curving his sculpted lips and creating grooves around the corners. *He's handsome, but not as handsome as Russell. I wonder how old he is.* For a moment, the extended lifespan of shifters blew Riley's mind, and she fell silent, trying to still her whirling thoughts.

"Sorry," she said, realizing she'd been staring again. "I really appreciate that." *Idiot, you're re-peating yourself.*

"Come and sit," Russell's father invited. "We have hot coffee and breakfast if you are hungry."

"Yes, thank you, Father," Russell agreed easily. "But stay there. I can take care of us. Riley." He indicated an armchair beside a small round wooden table. Riley removed her coat and hung it on a hook by the door, next to where Russ had left his while she was talking to his family. Then she perched on the chair he'd indicated. Russ moved into another room and returned with two plates balanced on his arm and a cup of coffee in each hand.

"Goodness, Russ," she said, startled by his balancing act, "I could have helped you with that. Were you ever a waiter?"

He laughed, setting a cup of coffee on each of two coasters on the little table before placing her plate in her lap. "No, never a waiter. I'd have to be a lot more social for that."

"Is this another bear thing?" she guessed as he sank into a matching chair across the table from her. The two of them sat at right angles to the sofa, where Randy and Russ' father sat in silence, regarding her with curiosity.

"Maybe," he replied. "I've never thought about it."

She grinned. “Okay then. This smells delicious.” She inhaled the fragrance of the bacon on her plate and her mouth watered. As Riley ate her breakfast, she observed Russell’s family. They sat in silence, not talking, laughing or even smiling, and yet there was a sense of calm acceptance around them. This was not an awkward silence that meant discomfort. Instead, these men had such internal peace that they had no need of words. It reminded her of life with her father. *Riley-girl, the world is full of chatter. But if you listen, underneath the noise is fear. There is no need to fear silence. It is in the place between words that understanding happens. Listen to the silence, Riley.*

She followed her father’s advice, not filling in the moment with words. Yes, she felt nervous, but she controlled her urge to chatter through it. And in time, she found she was able to relax somewhat, immerse herself partway in the day, though her busy mind never truly rested. She bundled up and followed her hosts to the meeting hall, a massive structure, also of evergreen logs, with bare walls. The strongest note of color in the room was the vibrant red and purple regalia some of the people wore. Others had on jeans and sweaters. In a place of honor, a rectangular shape sat draped in a purple woven cloth similar to the ones that decorated Russ' family home.

"What will happen?" Riley asked Russ, eyeing the covered coffin uncertainly.

"Lots of dancing," he replied. "Food and gifts. This is how we honor the deceased."

"I didn't bring a gift," she whispered urgently. "We didn't."

Russell turned to face her. "This tradition is different. Father will distribute gifts to the guests."

"Oh." Not sure what else to say, Riley fell back to silent observation. In later years, the images of the day would blend together. She ate moose meat and fry bread and drank what seemed like a gallon of black tea. People chanted and danced, waving sticks adorned with colorful – something she couldn't see clearly, while beating skin drums. The dancing seemed to consist of leaning forward and bobbing, perhaps stomping one foot. Though she was sure she could accomplish the steps, Riley feared committing a faux pas, and Russ assured her it was fine for her to watch. She ended up seated next to a lovely young woman about Riley's age.

"I wish I could join in the dancing," the young woman commented, patting her burgeoning belly. "But all the stomping makes me sore." Rummaging in a skin bag, she brought to light what appeared to be a folded piece of soft leather, which she laid in her lap. Another quick dig revealed a tiny pouch containing what turned out to be colorful beads and a needle. With skillful fingers, she began stringing the beads and attaching them to the leather.

"I bet," Riley said. "When are you due?"

"Any day now," the woman replied. "And you?"

Riley blushed. "I'm not sure I'm pregnant yet." Her fingertips trailed over her own nearly flat belly.

"You are," the woman said. "I'm assistant to the midwife. I know that look you have about you. You're glowing. I don't know you though. Are you from another village?"

Riley shook her head. "I... uh... my boyfriend is from here."

The woman's eyebrows drew together. "Who is your man?"

"Uh... Russell Tadzea."

The Den'a woman's puzzled expression broke into a wide grin. "My cousin! I had no idea he'd met someone, he keeps so much to himself. Congratulations. It will be so good for everyone when your child is born."

Talking about the child she was far from convinced she was having made Riley feel strange, like eels were swimming in her stomach – or maybe that was the moose meat – but the woman seemed not to notice.

"He's special, with his... mixed heritage. Not many of that sort. I'm so glad he's found a woman. Welcome to the family." Then she looked puzzled again. "What was your name?"

"Riley," she replied. "Riley Jenkins."

"Riley? What a funny name. I'm Nasnanna Tadzea."

Riley refrained from commenting that to her Nasnanna sounded much stranger than Riley. *When in Rome.*

Chanting, dancing, conversation, food. One hour blended into another until Riley almost felt comfortable at the Potlatch. While she knew she'd never actually be part of it, the people went out of their way to welcome her, once they figured out she was with Russ.

At night, she slept beside him in a narrow guest bed in his father's home. She stared at the bed and then as Russ, pressed close to the wall to make room for her. The chill in the room cut right through her pajamas and the thick red quilt sure looked inviting, not to mention her own personal mobile radiator.

"Come on, Riley," he urged. "It's another big day tomorrow. Get in."

She swallowed. "This doesn't seem right."

He sighed and grasped her hand, tugging her into the bed beside him. She lay stiff and uncomfortable as he settled into the space, snuggling close to her. He draped his arm over her waist and stroked her belly with his thumb. "Why are you so worried, honey? What doesn't seem right?"

"I don't know. Everyone knowing our business?" she whispered, not quite able to put her uneasy feelings into words.

Russell kissed her temple. "It's okay, you know. No one will mind. They know we belong to each other, and they understand the ways of my mother's people."

"So in everyone's mind we're married?" Riley demanded, not upset exactly, only trying to grasp an unfamiliar concept.

"Kind of," he replied. "I mean, everyone understands we're committed. They know, from so many generations of intermarrying with the bears, that if I say someone is my mate, it's for life. Now, if we decided to have some kind of wedding ceremony someday, no one would worry about that either. I think, in my case, people will just go along with whatever we decide."

She pondered the thought. Russell, it appeared, had other plans in mind. His stroking fingers slid upward, trying to cup the fullness of her breast. She stayed his hand with hers. "Now that I won't agree to. I'm sorry, honey. I just can't."

A soft, growling whine escaped Russell's throat.

"Not even if you make bear noises," she added.

Russell's muscular body sagged in disappointment. "We'll be here several more days, Riley-girl."

“And our cozy, private home is waiting for us when we leave,” she shot back, not budging an inch.

He sighed. “Women.”

Riley couldn’t help grinning. *If that’s what quarreling as a couple will be like, we can handle it, even if it doesn’t always go my way. Good thing Russ is willing to listen even when he doesn’t agree.* Then it sank in to her that they’d been intimate every single day since they moved in together, and most days before that. Spending a long, celibate weekend in bed with her lover went from being a necessity to an almost unattainable goal in a single heartbeat. But the thought that Russ’ father or brother might think they were… doing it… bothered her too much. So she tried to settle down and sleep, and eventually Russ’ warmth and the familiar rhythm of his soft snores lulled her to sleep.

Chapter 10

The next day, Russell snagged Riley away from the gathering shortly after lunch, wrapped her in her outerwear and walked her across the village to a small, low structure. Inside, an elderly woman waited. She had a round figure and wore a long, thick button-up sweater. A silver braid hung over her shoulder. Beside her, the young pregnant woman Riley had met sat at a desk, typing on a computer.

"Riley, this is Mrs. Forrest. She's the village's healer and midwife. Nasnanna mentioned she thought you might be expecting. Given everything... about me, I thought it might be a good idea for you to see the midwife here. I have no idea, if you are, whether there might be what look like abnormalities to a human, but that are normal to someone of mixed genetics...." He stammered to a halt.

"I think we should have talked about this before you dragged me here," Riley said in a dry voice, giving her boyfriend a sour look. "It's too soon to tell if I'm pregnant, and I think a pee stick would suffice to begin with."

"It might not be too soon," the old woman said in a soft and carefully enunciated voice. "We have better tests than that stick. Will you let us find out? It is good to know."

Riley sighed. "Fine. What do you need to do?"

"When was your last menstrual period?" Nasnanna asked.

Riley thought back. Then she bit her lip. "It might not be as 'too soon' as I thought. I finished just before Thanksgiving."

Nasnanna smirked and made a note on the chart.

"Well then," Mrs. Forrest said, "the stick will work."

Riley couldn't really articulate why the sight of this traditional looking woman rummaging in a white cabinet and emerging with a sample cup and two disinfecting wipes struck her as odd. *Guess my sheltered childhood is showing. Time to grow up, Riley.* It did make her feel a bit better that modern medical techniques seemed to be the norm.

Within minutes she had the cup prepared and left it in the bathroom, returning to Russ, who was sitting in the waiting area, leafing through a copy of Field and Stream.

The two midwives moved to the back portion of the clinic, through a door with heavy wood grain.

As Riley sank into her seat, Russell looked up, meeting her eyes.

"It's probably positive," she said, and despite the inevitability of it, her heart began to pound.

"I know," he replied.

"The principals aren't going to like this." Worry clamped down on Riley. "Do you think they'll fire me?"

"For taking maternity leave in the fall? Nah." He set the magazine aside and took her hand. "People who hire young women have to expect to deal with things like this. I promise, it won't be a big deal. Just be sure your lesson plans are ready, but you'll have the whole summer to work on them."

Riley nodded. "Do you know a good babysitter or anything? I'm not sure I can afford that on my salary."

"Riley, honey, you're not exactly a single mom," Russell reminded her. "I'm in this for life, no matter what. Besides, my work schedule is flexible. I can watch the little one when you're at work. Even bring her to you at your lunch break to nurse, if you'd like."

Riley blinked away a sudden burn in her eyes. His talk of bringing a baby to her and nursing made the whole thing even more real. It was one thing intentionally to risk pregnancy by not using protection. It was another to know that the inevitable had already happened. *Because it has. Everyone realizes it.*

"I'm scared," she whispered.

"I know, honey. I'm not surprised. But I'm here. I'll always be here. You're safe with me, Riley."

She leaned over the arms of their respective chairs, ignoring the metal that pressed uncomfortably into her hip, and rested her head on his shoulder. He wrapped one brawny arm around her back and stroked her. “It’s okay, Riley,” he murmured.

Nasnanna returned to the room a minute or so later and said tartly, “I don’t need to tell you the results. You already know.”

Riley nodded against Russ’ sweater.

“So, given everything, Mrs. Forrest and I think we should be your primary caregivers. We can handle all prenatal including ultrasounds, bloodwork, everything, as well as deliveries. And in case you were worried, I’m a registered nurse, so you’ll be getting ‘modern’ medicine in addition to traditional wisdom.”

“I never said otherwise,” Riley stated.

“I saw your face,” the young nurse insisted.

“Yes,” Riley admitted with a sigh. “Forgive me a moment of doubt, okay? This is all a bit overwhelming.”

“Nasnanna,” Russell added in an ursine rumble. “I will not have Riley stressed during her pregnancy. If you pick on her, I *will* take her to someone else. She’s had so many huge changes to her life lately. Don’t push it.”

Nasnanna took a deep breath. Under her unbuttoned lab coat, her own baby squirmed visibly through her scrubs, making the wolves and bears printed on the thin fabric seem to dance on a snowy background. Riley gulped. *I'm in for it now.*

"All right," Nasnanna said with a sigh. "I get it. We'll consider this a non-event, shall we? And move forward as we would with any other person?"

Russ started to growl, but Riley held up a hand. "I agree."

"Well then, we'll start by assuming you're approximately eight weeks. An ultrasound next month will help with that determination. We'll need to do bloodwork and eventually discuss a birth plan. If you don't have any complications, we'd suggest you deliver here. Golden doesn't have anything like our centuries of accumulated experience. Plus, their doctor knows nothing of shape shifters, of course, and if the baby shows any exceptionalities, they might think it's an emergency and off you'd go. Having to be transported to Fairbanks because of a non-existent emergency wouldn't be fun."

"I think here would be fine," Riley replied.

Mrs. Forrest opened the door to the back room. "Please come, Riley," she intoned. "We need to draw blood."

Riley rolled her eyes. *I hate needles.* "Okay, I'm coming."

* * *

That night, her arm bandaged and her mind swirling, Riley sat out another dance. As she watched her beloved's clan chant and stomp, she tried to focus her thoughts. It was no use. Feeling overwhelmed by life, she rested her forehead in her hand and closed her eyes.

"Riley?" a female voice drew her back to reality.

"Nasnanna," Riley replied a bit coolly, not sure where she stood with the Den'a woman.

"I'm sorry I got snippy earlier," she said, eyes downcast. "I didn't mean to be so touchy. It's just… you know…"

"I know," Riley replied. "There are rednecks in the world. And maybe my reaction was a bit… unflattering. Not to mention unfounded. After all, midwives have been delivering healthy babies for millennia, way before modern medicine. It just took me a minute to remember. I swear I wasn't trying to put down you, Mrs. Forrest, or this community in any way. I just got a bit... nervous."

"First pregnancies are scary," Nasnanna agreed, patting her own belly. "I can certainly relate. So are we good?"

Riley nodded. "I think we can chalk it all up to a miscommunication."

"Sounds good." Nasnanna grinned, showing straight white teeth. Then she let out a little squeak. "Stop that, you," she addressed her belly, shoving at a limb that pressed her belly out in what looked like a painful move.

"Does that hurt?" Riley asked, alarmed at the young woman's rapidly changing shape.

"Yes," Nasnanna replied bluntly. "It hurts every day. I can't sleep and I can hardly hold my pee. This is natural, though. It helps overcome any fear of delivery. I'm so ready, I don't care if it hurts to give birth. That's nature's way."

"I see," Riley replied.

"I know it's a lot to take in," the young woman added, "but you'll get through. It'll be fine. And soon I'll have my little boy in my arms, and it will all be worthwhile. You will too."

Riley smiled. "Where's his father? I'd like to meet a few more people here."

Nasnanna scowled. "Afghanistan," she replied, pouting. "Can you imagine? He's a Marine. I told him he would melt like a snowman in the Middle East, but he didn't listen. So he's going to miss his son's birth. Thank goodness for Skype."

Yikes, Riley thought. *No wonder she's a little grumpy.*

"Do you have anyone to help you after the delivery?" she asked. *If Russ wasn't here, I'd be completely alone.*

"Yes. My mother lives next door to me, and Mrs. Forrest is my aunt, so we should be fine."

"I'm glad to hear that."

"Say," Nasnanna said, suddenly changing the subject, "would you like to know more about the dance they're doing right now?"

"Yes," Riley agreed immediately. "I'd like that very much."

Chapter 11

"Work tomorrow," Riley thought, stretching out in the bed she now thought of as hers. Her body still tingled in the aftermath of her welcome home celebration with Russell. He'd made sure she knew how much he'd missed her, even though she'd slept beside him every night.

Riley shivered. Every inch of her skin had been marked with gentle bites and burning kisses. Her lips felt swollen and inside… sore was only the beginning. And yet, the pleasure had been intense, and she hadn't held back from screaming her ecstasy to the rafters. *I've been ridden hard,* she thought, enjoying the afterglow.

Half-drowsing, she scarcely registered movement beside her until the cold crept through the now half-empty bed and nipped at her.

Riley's eyes snapped open. *It's late. The bathroom light is still off. Where on earth did Russ go?*

Rising from the bed, she trailed to the window and looked outside. A huge full moon hung low above the trees and cast golden light like spilled honey across the night-dark snow. Movement to the left drew her gaze. Russell stood outside, wearing only his jeans and sweater. The sight of his bare feet sinking into the snow made Riley's toes ache in sympathy. From the trees a massive white shape lumbered into the clearing heading straight for her beloved. While she knew he should be safe from bears, it still made her stomach knot. She laid a hand over the secret place where their baby rested.

The bear rose to its hind legs, towering over Russ' human form. A roar set the treetops shuddering. He responded. *As long as I live, I will never get used to that sound coming from his human throat.*

The bear shook, became hazy, and seemed to shrink in on itself. In the blink of an eye, a man with white hair and golden skin stood naked before Russell. The two men stared at each other for a moment. From her angle, she could only see her beloved's back, but he seemed to be gesturing. Then he half-turned, indicating the window in which she stood. Riley sank back into the shadows, but continued to watch.

The strange shifter froze, then clapped Russell on the shoulder so hard he staggered. Laughing roars rolled across the meadow. The men stayed together another minute before the stranger shimmered back into a bear and loped away into the trees. Russell turned to the window and waved. Then he stripped off his clothes and before she could draw a breath, a second bear ran into the woods.

Blushing at having been caught, Riley slunk back into bed, pulled the covers up to her chin and closed her eyes.

* * *

Home feels strange. Why? I grew up here. What's so strange about this? She scanned the walls of her father's study. *Perhaps the mess.* Her father's beloved books had been knocked from the shelves and strewn around the room. His desk sported deep gouges and cuts she'd never seen before. One of the diamond shaped panes was cracked and the door hung crooked, its upper hinges disconnected. Anxiety knotted her belly as the reason for the disarray hit home.

She stepped away from the desk and into the shadow of a bookshelf, hoping to become invisible to anyone who might come into the room. Too late. A hand thick with scars clamped down on her wrist, and at the sight of the tattooed knuckles, she felt a strong urge to vomit. *It's a dream, Riley. He can't hurt you in a dream.* But she didn't know, determined as Danny was to control her, whether any damage might turn out to be real.

"Little sister," a cold, expressionless voice hissed in her ear, "where is it?"

Riley ground her teeth. "Where's what?" she asked, yanking at his arm and trying to get her wrist free.

"You know," he replied. "You tried to cheat me, little girl. I won't stand for it."

Riley's whole body felt icy cold. "Cheat you how? I gave you my entire inheritance. What more can you possibly want? You can't have my paychecks. I earn those, and I need them."

"Liar," he roared, and she flinched, inching as far away from him as his bruising grip would allow. "You know what I want. You give it to me now!"

"I have no idea what you're talking about," she insisted. "I'm not lying, I swear. There's nothing left. He wasn't even your father, and you have it all."

In a heartbeat his face transformed from rage to calm, but the glitter in his eyes caused a thrill of terror to shoot through her. He slowly closed his free hand into a fist and let her get a good look at it. "Are you sure you don't want to reconsider that position?" He drew his arm back.

"There's nothing to tell," she insisted, nearly shrieking.

The fist flew, but Riley, for the first time in her life, dodged. The blow hit her hip, bruising deep into the soft flesh, but protecting her vulnerable belly from his rage. *You'll never touch me there again. I have something to protect now.* While he stared, startled by her unexpected resistance, she jerked her wrist in the direction of his fingertips and managed to break his hold. Stomping down hard on his foot, she made a run for it, racing past him and through the broken door of the study. His pounding footsteps demonstrated how quickly he'd recovered. Riley's feet seemed to grow wings as she put on an extra burst of speed, desperate to put space between her dangerous half-brother and her unborn baby. "Wake up, Riley," she begged herself. "Wake up and you'll be safe."

"You'll never be safe from me," he laughed, and she could feel his hot breath on her neck. "I'll find you no matter where you hide. I'll get what's mine."

A vicious cramp tightened down in Riley's flank, but she dared not slow down. Sobbing with pain and fear, she clutched at it.

A familiar, full-throated roar rattled the bungalow from foundation to ridgepole.

"What the hell?" Danny demanded no one in particular, stopping to stare at the enormous white creature galloping their direction on pigeon-toed paws the size of his face. "You have weird dreams, Riley."

She laughed hysterically. Part of Danny's danger was that he genuinely didn't realize how scary he was… except when he was trying to be. It was as though more than one person lived inside his oversized thug body.

"That's not all I have," she snarled. This time her own fist flew, connecting solidly with Danny's throat.

He croaked like a frog and staggered to the side. Riley ran straight toward the bear. "I can't wake up, Russ. Help me!"

She could have sworn he nodded a moment before those huge paws wrapped around her body. Fur faded to flesh and she opened her eyes to find herself in bed with Russell holding her in his arms. Her side ached and her hip throbbed. She clung to her lover, heart pounding, as terror slowly released her from its grip. Tears streaked down her cheeks and she sobbed against his bare shoulder.

Russell held her while she cried, making wordless rumbling noises that almost sounded like purring. When at last her adrenaline had been shed and she lay in a trembling, boneless heap under the heavy quilt, he spoke. "You didn't tell me Danny was a dreamwalker too."

"I didn't know," she mumbled. "I've had nightmares about him my whole life, but until tonight, I never knew they were real."

"Too real," he replied, tossing back the covers to reveal her hip, where a huge red mark was slowly turning purple. "If he had hit…" Russell's big hand splayed on her belly. She could hear his teeth grinding. His fingers dug into her skin.

"I wouldn't let that happen," she insisted, drawing away from his too-intense touch. "I know what's at stake. I know how Danny moves, what he does."

"Not good enough," Russell said darkly. "If you die in the dream, you die for real. Where do you think those legends come from? If anything happened to you, Riley, it would be the end of me. You have to protect yourself. You have to block him from entering your dreams."

Riley's labored breathing was beginning to slow, as was her heartbeat. Snuggled safe in the arms of her bear, she had to acknowledge the truth of what he was saying.

"You're right." The fragrance of Russell – of fresh cold air and warm, vital man filled her. "How do I prevent it from happening? I didn't mean to let him at all. I just wanted to sleep. I'm so tired all the time, you know? I need a good night's sleep."

"You're going to be tired tomorrow," he said. "Nightmares are no more restful than being awake."

"I know." The clock on the bedside table read 2:00 am. Riley yawned. "How do I make sure he can't find me? This was too close." She trailed her fingertips over her hip.

"For tonight, let me watch over you. I can protect you awake or asleep. Later, when you're rested, we'll figure out a way to guard your dreams. Let's plan that for the weekend, okay?"

"Okay."

Warmed and soothed by Russell's powerful presence, and reassured by the knowledge that he could guard her dreams as well as her waking moments, Riley succumbed to fatigue and fell into a dead sleep.

* * *

"Are you kidding me?" Riley asked, staring at a building that in no way resembled the rest of Golden. The small, single-story space stood out sharply against the gray plastic siding and red brick buildings on its sides. This place seemed to have been constructed out of decommissioned ship's hull boards. The front of the building curved like the bottom of a ship too. Each individual board had been painted a different color. Starting at the ground, a band of purple lightened to blue, then green, orange, yellow, and the roof had been shingled in red. Two huge display windows were framed in multicolored shutters that mirrored the pattern of the structure. Inside the windows to the left of the bright green front door, three ancient and dusty books reclined on a purple velvet cloth. On the right, the entire display had been converted into a planter and filled with green sprouts. A heating lamp hung above. A sign in the window advertised wheat grass shots for $1 each.

"Yeah, why not?" Russell asked. "I told you people in Alaska were different. Now, listen. Before you get any funny ideas, Samantha is trained as a physicist. If you want to get dizzy, forget her herbal concoctions and just ask her to explain the quantum nature of the empath phenomenon. She really knows her stuff."

"I've seen New Age shops before," Riley said. "Portland has a few. And I've been to Seattle as well. I just didn't expect to find one here."

"Well, you did," Russell replied. His grin made her want to kiss him. "Shall we go inside? See what she recommends to protect your dreams?"

"Yes," Riley agreed easily. Hand in hand with her beloved, they entered the one-room shop.

As she expected, the inside was just as unusual as the outside. One entire wall had been converted into a set of narrow shelves clustered with tiny bottles. Below each one, a printed label described the contents, from acacia to yucca. The back wall, opposite the door, had been turned into a long counter. One end supported the press where the wheatgrass shots were produced. A tray held several tiny glasses. A bucket on the floor appeared to be for spent glasses, though today it stood empty. On the other side, the cash register awaited a sale. The wall opposite the apothecary was completely covered in bookshelves.

In the center of the room, a woman with blond hair and striking blue eyes sat at a table. The purple sequined tablecloth matched a scarf tying back her hair. She wore a black power suit. The sight of her made Riley smile, in spite of her fatigue and nervousness.

"Hello, Russ," the woman said.

"Amy," Russell returned the greeting.

"And you're Riley, right? The new kindergarten teacher?"

Riley nodded, already used to people who had nothing to do with the school recognizing her. *Golden is a small town after all.*

"What can I do for you two today?" Amy asked. "Take a seat and let's talk. You both look stressed."

"Riley is a dreamwalker," Russell said bluntly, urging her into a seat.

Amy's big blue eyes widened to alarming proportions. "Are you sure?" She turned to Riley.

"I guess so," Riley replied. "I've had the same dream as Russell many times."

"Oh, interesting," the woman said. "So, what's the problem?"

Riley shot Russ a pleading look. He acknowledged her request with a twist of his lips. "Riley has been threatened in the dream. A man from her past stalks her there, tries to harm her."

"Are you sure he's not just dreaming?" Amy suggested. "Sometimes one person's recurring dreams can seem like a metaphysical meeting to another."

Riley shook her head. "If you could see the bruise he gave me..." *I wish Russ hadn't described him that way. Danny is my brother, not a former lover.*

Amy touched her hand. "That's very dangerous, Riley. If you're both so present in the dream that he can hurt you physically, you're in a precarious position."

"More than you know," Riley mumbled.

Amy gave her a questioning look.

Riley sighed. They wouldn't be able to keep the secret much longer anyway. "I'm pregnant. I don't want Danny to hurt my baby."

"That's a real concern," Amy said, her lips pinching tight shut. "Jealousy and all."

Riley rolled her eyes. "Danny is my brother. Keep that in mind."

"Oh." Amy blinked.

"He's still a crazy and dangerous asshole though, and I want him out of my dreams. Can you help me?"

"Of course!" Amy agreed. "Let me think. I'm not a dreamwalker myself. I'm more into herbal concoctions and crystals. These have a long history of traditional uses that can be investigated and proven, at least in an anecdotal way. I think we need to start with personal protection and then move outward to the bedroom and the entire home. Eventually you'll need to see an experienced dreamwalker who can guide you in how to guard your dreams." Then she turned to Russell. "Can't you help her?"

Russ considered. "I'd have to look up some theories. I've never encountered anything like a targeted threat there. My father is investigating who to ask. He wasn't sure either."

Amy nodded. "Okay. In the meanwhile, let me think. How can we block your dreams from unwanted intruders…?" Amy tapped her fingernail on her front teeth. Then she rose from the chair and began whirling around the shop like a tiny blond tornado. Zipping behind the counter, she disappeared for a moment and rummaged in the embedded display case, returning with a long silver chain from which dangled a silver filigree pendant contained a smooth, matte black stone.

"This is black jasper," Amy informed her. "Wear it all the time. It's highly protective as well as healing. If your brother has been hurting you for a long time, you need it. It's rumored to bring good luck in all kinds of fights, and blocking your brother out of your dreams will be a spiritual battle, for sure."

Riley accepted the necklace and hung it around her neck.

"Let me think... Okay!" Amy raced to the apothecary shelves. Removing a little bottle, she shook a few small brown nuggets into her hand and carried them back to the counter. Another quick rummage brought out an electric hot plate, on which she set a glass vessel. Dumping her handful of herbs into it, she added liquid from a bottle labeled 'blessed water,' and turned on the heat. "Rinse with this decoction of burdock roots. It will help you heal negative feelings about yourself. I'm sure that's part of the problem, right?"

Riley sighed. "Yeah, it is. I feel like such a wuss."

"You're not," Amy assured her, and Russell reached across the table to squeeze her hand. "Your brother worked hard to demoralize you, both waking and sleeping, am I right?" At Riley's nod, she continued. "That's bound to have a deep impact on your self-image. It's not your fault, but you do need to deal with it. To strengthen your psyche. You're not under his thumb anymore."

"Okay, I'll buy that," Riley replied.

"Now, to deal with the sleep issues. A pillow filled with protective herbs is a good start. Russell, could you get me an empty pillow from the compartment under the left side window?"

Riley followed her boyfriend's movements with her eyes. Sure enough, under the big windows at the front of the store, a set of drawers, four on each side, had been filled with – Riley didn't know what. But when Russell rose from rummaging in the uppermost one, he held a small ecru-colored sack. "Is this it?"

"Yes," Amy agreed. He handed it to her. Riley rose from her seat and joined them back at the herbs display. "Agrimony," Amy began, shaking a few dried leaves into the sack. The fabric, which appeared to be unbleached cotton, had been fully stitched on three sides and half stitched on the fourth, leaving a small aperture into which Amy concocted her sleep protection recipe. "This will dispel negative influences. Anise to prevent disturbing dreams. Balsam to break up negativity. Bergamot to stop interference and promote restful sleep. You'll need that with the pregnancy anyway. Blue violet for sleep as well. Catnip to protect you while you're asleep." With a speed that astonished Riley, Amy moved along the alphabetized shelves, sprinkling one herb after another into the pillow. Then she headed back to the drawers at the front of the shop and removed a container, pouring its contents into the pillow. "Buckwheat hulls are for financial prosperity, but they're nice to sleep on."

"Hey," Riley said, "financial prosperity would be welcome too." They all laughed.

At last, Amy returned to the table and with a few deft twitches of a needle she seemed to have pulled from the fabric wrapped around her hair, she closed the aperture and handed the pillow to Amy. "See how you like that."

Concerned of the effect all those herbs might have on her sense of smell, which pregnancy had rendered so sensitive that the odor of the mop water the school custodians used made her gag, she took a cautious sniff. Mellow citrus, pine and licorice smells blended appealingly together along with a peppery sweetness. Riley burrowed her face into it and inhaled deeply. A sense of calm washed over her. "I love it."

"Careful," Russ urged. "Don't fall asleep sitting up." He grabbed the pillow and sniffed. "That smells okay."

"Glad you both like it. Now for something to sprinkle around for protection." This time Amy retrieved a plastic sack and again began shaking in herbs, still explaining what she was doing until the terms and definitions swam in Riley's mind. "Angelica as a barrier to negativity – lots of that. Basil for positivity and strength. Boneset to get rid of evil and negativity. Calendula for protection and good dreams." Soon the bag was filled with a mixture of gray-green sprigs and faded flowers. "Sprinkle two thick lines of this under the bed, in a circle without a break to create a double shield against any threatening influence. Nothing should be inside your dreams except the two of you. I'd also recommend making a cross at each corner of the house with it, in case you fall asleep on the sofa or something. I'll mark down the recipe and make a big batch so you can get more. Replenish it frequently."

Russ and Riley both nodded. He looked as startled as she felt by the whirlwind of information.

"And one more thing. I'll make a mixture to burn. Sprinkle this in your fire tonight to cleanse any existing negativity from your home." Amy hurried back to her herbs, muttering to herself. "Ague root for protection... alkanet for a positive influence... Althea root to attract good spirits... More angelica."

By the time they had paid for their purchases and wandered into the street, Riley's head was spinning. Russ looked equally startled. They walked in silence, their purchases clutched in a small fabric bag of undyed cotton, with pale green handles, which dangled from Riley's arm. As they neared the snowmobile, Riley finally managed to ask Russ a question.

"Why didn't you just tell her Danny was my brother?"

"I don't know," Russ said. "I guess I'm just naturally secretive. I don't tell people more than they need to know."

"Oh," Riley said. Then they both fell silent again. Tucking the bag into the compartment under the seat, they mounted the sled and headed home.

Chapter 12

By spring break, Riley had reached approximately her sixteenth week of pregnancy. With her brother no longer haunting her dreams, she felt better overall. The nausea had been brief and not too bothersome, and she had just received positive formative evaluations at work. Apparently, the school and the parents were happy enough with her, which helped her relax also. Spring break found her back at the Den'a village, lying on the examination table in the back room of Mrs. Forrest's clinic, with her sweater tucked up around her breasts as the midwife poked at her belly.

"I think I should do an ultrasound," the midwife suggested. "You seem anxious, Russell. This can set your mind at ease."

"Mine too," Riley added. "I want to be sure I'm carrying a baby and not a cub… or a litter of cubs."

Mrs. Forrest laughed, a dry chuckle. "Yes. That would be good to know. So you agree to the ultrasound?"

Riley tried not to squeal as the elderly Native woman squeezed icy cold gel on her belly.

"How is Nasnanna?" Riley asked to take her mind off the uncomfortable sensation.

"She's well," the taciturn woman replied. "Her son was born three days after the Potlatch. His father came home to see him. The baby eats well and Nasnanna will be back at work soon."

"Will her mother watch him?" Riley asked.

Mrs. Forrest lifted a plastic… thingy that looked like it came from the Starship Enterprise and pressed it low on Riley's belly, sliding it through the thick goop until she picked up an image.

"She will bring him with her until he is old enough not to need milk every few hours. Tiny ones are easy enough to bring along. Look, can you see that?"

Riley fell silent. The ultrasound showed a soft and rapid pulsing. She gasped. "Is that the heartbeat?"

"Yes," the old woman replied. "It's strong. Your baby looks healthy."

"Thank goodness." Russell squeezed Riley's hand. He'd been hovering constantly in the two months since her brother had invaded her dream, worried the unfortunate incident had harmed their baby.

"Here, look," Mrs. Forrest suggested, indicating the screen. Riley bit her lip as her heart melted. On the screen a small and skinny shape danced and waved tiny limbs. The midwife clicked her mouse and the image froze. "Look," she said again. "See those lines?"

She indicated the shadowy picture.

"Yes," Riley said slowly. She could see it, but wasn't sure what it meant.

"It's a girl."

Riley's jaw dropped. She turned to Russell, hoping with everything she had that he wouldn't be disappointed. Her heart turned over when she saw the watery grin on his face.

"A girl," he breathed. He leaned over Riley and kissed her forehead. "Thank you, love."

"You're happy then?" she asked stupidly.

"Yes, so happy, honey." He kissed her again.

"Look," Mrs. Forrest urged them for the third time. Riley turned her eyes from Russell's and her breath caught as the flailing limb approached the little girl's face and she tucked her thumb into her mouth. Riley exhaled in a soft squeak.

"That's so sweet," Russell breathed.

Riley laid her hand on his cheek and drew him down to kiss his lips. "I love you, Russ. Thank you for our daughter."

He didn't speak, but the burning gaze he turned on her was answer enough.

* * *

That night, Riley slept badly, troubled by unsettling dreams. It felt as though some sort of beast was prowling around the edges of her consciousness, looking for a way into the protected area she'd erected. She was tempted to reform the igloo where she'd hidden for so many years.

Instead, she woke herself up and discovered she was alone in the bed again. This time, the emptiness of the cabin struck her more sharply than the cold. The eerie feeling that she was not actually by herself gnawed at her, and she scrutinized the window, imagining all sorts of glaring ogres in the impenetrable darkness. Terrified, she closed her eyes tight against the threatening shadows, but without her vision to focus her attention on reality, the unseen thing that stalked her mind tugged at her, trying to draw her into its snare.

"I know where you are," Danny's voice echoed across the dreamscape that somehow could touch her waking mind. "I'll find you and take what's mine. You can't fight me. You can't escape me. I am always here."

The bed jostled violently and a frozen hand closed on Riley's shoulder. She screamed, flailing and managed to connect a solid blow against a wall of muscular flesh.

"Riley," a familiar voice murmured in a soothing rumble. "Riley, it's me. You're okay."

"Russell?" She turned, trembling, into his arms.

"Hush, Riley. Hush. What happened?"

"He's trying to find me," she sobbed. "He's searching for me. He's trying to get into my dreams and he said he knows where I am!"

Russell's muscles flexed. "He shouldn't be able to touch your dreams, Riley. And how could he know where you are?"

"There's a paper trail, I'm sure. I didn't try to hide from him." Her voice wavered and broke on every word. "I thought once he had my inheritance he'd leave me alone. He thinks I have something, Russ. Something he wants." She shuddered. Nausea rose up in her belly and she gagged.

"Whoa there," Russell exclaimed. "Up you go, Riley-girl." Russell half-supported, half-carried Riley to the en suite quickly, gathering her hair back. She retched into the toilet and then moaned, throat burning and belly cramping.

When the spasm passed, Russell sank to the floor and pulled Riley onto his lap. He rocked her slowly back and forth. "Poor girl. That must have been one hell of a nightmare. But, honey, even if he does find you, how do you think he'll get through me? I may look like an ordinary man right now, but you know if you're threatened, Danny will face ten feet and one thousand pounds of claws, teeth and muscle. I won't let him hurt you. I can tear him to pieces and no one would ever know."

His words cut deep into Riley. Both the truth and the awareness that the man she loved was not exactly a man. He had different rules, a different moral code than most men. At least, most American men. Conditioned to deal with his own threats rather than resorting to the police, he would kill without hesitation. *He already has,* she thought, recalling the bearskin in front of the fire. *He already wants revenge for what Danny has done to me. He won't hesitate.* Hating the violence even as she reveled in the feeling of complete safety, Riley nestled closer to her man.

"How did I get so lucky?" she asked, her head on his chest.

"I'm the lucky one, Riley. Can you stand up?" He helped her to her feet and filled a paper cup from the sink. "Drink this, and then brush your teeth. It's time to go back to bed. You have another big work day tomorrow."

Riley drained the cup and scrubbed her mouth with toothpaste, wanting to rid herself of the vile taste of vomit. Then she let Russell lead her back to the bed. He tucked her under the covers and then crouched down on his hands and knees.

"What are you doing?" she asked sleepily.

"Checking the herb rings. Ah, one's broken here." He scrabbled briefly and then emerged, sliding under the covers beside Riley and pulling her close. "I guess one of us must have erased part of the ring with our foot. We'll have to be careful. I need the mother of my baby to get plenty of rest. No wearing yourself out, Riley."

She pressed herself directly against Russell's body, savoring his warmth. "Okay, boss."

"That's right, little girl," he teased.

She could feel his muscles relaxing now that she had regained her control. "Are you sure we're safe?"

"Of course, love. What could touch us here? Sleep, Riley."

His kiss on her cheek comprised her last conscious thought.

Chapter 13

Despite Russell's assurances, Riley continued to feel an increasing sense of emotional discomfort. Each night she checked to be sure that the circles drawn under the bed remained undisturbed. And yet, despite her precautions, she could still feel Danny's threatening presence just beyond her dreams, pressing, testing the defenses. He wanted to get to her, and every time he was thwarted, his rage grew. So great was Riley's anxiety, it began to affect her waking hours as well. Though she felt secure enough at work, in town surrounded by people, the isolation of Russell's cabin no longer seemed like a safeguard for anything more than his privacy – and the privacy of any ill-intentioned person who wanted to come their way. If Russell stepped outside for one of his bear rambles in the woods, she remained awake and alert until he returned, which took a toll on her. Though only two weeks had passed since her nightmare, the harrowing anxiety and lack of sleep had etched marks on her face – dark circles under her eyes, pallor and that haunted expression she used to wear had returned. She looked like a wraith.

She could see in Russell's face that her worry upset him. Instead of wild sex, they now spent hours cuddling, as he tried to remind her she was worrying needlessly.

When Russell picked her up after a long day of work followed by an evening of parent-teacher conferences, she seemed to be drooping on her feet.

"Will you be able to hold on?" he asked as he unchained the snowmobile and tucked the lock into the compartment under the seat.

She nodded wearily.

"This isn't good, Riley. You look like you're going to fall over." Russ turned his back to his vehicle, and hugged her. "Tomorrow, I want you to call in sick. I'm taking you to the Den'a village to see the midwife and my father. Someone has to be able to help you relax. Okay?"

"I hate to waste the sick day," she protested. "I'll only get twenty as it is. That's two weeks unpaid."

"I don't care," he snapped. "It's not like we're broke. If you can't relax, you're going to miss a lot more than that. You'll end up stuck in bed."

Riley sniffled, knowing he was right. "Okay," she said in a wavering voice.

Russell gave her a long look. Then without a word he tightened his arms around her, rubbing her back. "Maybe we're both making too big a deal out of this. Mrs. Forrest should be able to give us some information."

"I hope so. Not sleeping well is making me hysterical," she admitted.

"I bet. Poor Riley. Come on, let's go home."

At the thought of their home, which had once seemed so appealing, Riley had to suppress a shudder. *I don't want to be there. It's not safe.* But she knew the thought was irrational, and so she climbed onto the snowmobile behind Russell and locked her arms around his waist, leaning her head on his parka and closing her eyes for the long ride into the woods.

The scent of pine and fresh air soothed her nerves, and the familiar hum of the engine nearly lulled her to sleep. Here, far from her protective rituals and safeguards, the haunting voice seemed to whisper directly in her ear, "I almost have you. And I'll have what's mine. You can't hide it from me forever."

Riley jerked herself upright and almost fell from the sled, only to discover that they were parked outside the cabin. She rose unsteadily and staggered. As always, Russ had his arms around her, supporting her. "You okay?"

"I guess," she replied. "I think I dozed off on the sled."

His dark eyes turned tender. "You must be exhausted. Let me make dinner, okay, Riley? You rest."

Though part of her wanted to protest, to offer to cook together as they enjoyed doing so often, her weary body answered for her. "Okay," she agreed, defeated. "I appreciate that."

"Let's get you inside before you tip over," Russ suggested. Carefully he walked her through the door and settled her on the sofa. Riley tucked a pillow under her head and went completely limp while Russell puttered around in the kitchen.

"It stinks in here," he commented. "I'll take out the trash."

Riley couldn't smell anything, she was too busy fighting sleep to worry about some smelly garbage. The last thing she wanted was to hear Danny's teasing whispers. They filled her with such anxiety, and she couldn't banish the thought that he wanted to find her, was trying to find her. *Will find me.* She shivered. Despite her best efforts, she must have drifted off briefly, because the scent of toasting bread teased her back to full awareness.

"Russell?"

He stood before her faster than she would have thought possible.

"What do you need, honey?"

"Can you get me my dad's book please?"

He quirked one eyebrow, but stalked into the bedroom nonetheless, returning with the battered and ink stained tome, which he handed to her. Touching the ragged cover made her feel a bit better.

"Thank you. What are you making, by the way?"

"Grilled cheese and soup."

She smiled wanly. "That sounds perfect."

Russell kissed her forehead. "I aim to please, milady," he teased, drawing a tired chuckle from Riley. She cupped his cheek and drew him down for another kiss. His lips caressed hers with irresistible sweetness. Riley closed her eyes. "I love you, Russ. I'm sorry to be such a lazybones today."

"Lazybones," he snorted. "You must be joking. Listen, Riley, you worked hard today, on your feet, chasing little kids around, right?"

She nodded.

"Then you stayed extra late and talked to parents, right?"

Again she bowed her head in a weary nod.

"And you're hungry and exhausted from not sleeping well. And you're pregnant – with my baby, I might add. What part of that is lazy if you let me make you dinner tonight?"

He didn't say another word. Didn't have to. He just kissed her lips and headed back to the kitchen to tend the sandwiches before they burned.

Riley lay back on the sofa, her mind blank, staring at the ceiling while the scents of the food wafted over her. She seemed to drift again, not to sleep, but near it. So near she could feel the beast that had been caged outside her consciousness pacing and prodding, looking for a way in.

"Russell?"

"Yes, love?" He suddenly stood before her, holding out a mug and a plate. Riley let out a little yip of surprise.

"Sorry." He set the mug down on the coaster, retrieved her father's book and set it aside as well before handing her the plate, cupping her shoulder in one hand and helping her to plump up a pillow behind her back so she could lean on the sofa's wooden arm. She could feel his intense body heat even through her layers of clothing. "What is it?"

"How does he do what he does?"

"Hmmm. Be right back." Russ returned to the kitchen. When his own food had been situated at the coffee table on the other end of the sofa, he sat down beside Riley and lifted her ankles, setting her feet in his lap. She took a bite of her sandwich and savored the experience of the simple food. Hot, crunchy buttery bread. Smooth, rich melted cheese. Perfection. Then she swallowed and asked her question again.

"How does Danny get into my dreams?"

Russell considered as he drank soup from a mug. "He must have the same ability I do," he answered at last.

"But you said you can't do that," she reminded him. "You told me that back when we first got together."

Russell's mouth quirked on one side, though the movement in no way resembled a smile. "I said I don't do that, if you recall. I can, but it's rude, not to mention illegal, at least under the laws of my father's people. Entering someone's mind without permission is something like rape." Then he realized what he'd just said and made an even less happy face.

Riley felt no offense. "You're not wrong. It does feel like a violation. Not what we do," she clarified quickly, lest he misunderstand. "You've asked permission to share my dreams. And sending messages this way is quite convenient, but that's the thing, Russ. From the beginning, you've asked what I wanted and respected my decisions. Danny has been forcing his way into my mind for months now."

The food seemed to be having a revivifying effect on Riley, so she was able to set her empty plate aside, retrieving her mug and taking a swallow of salty broth with rice.

"Probably longer than that," Russell admitted, with a pained expression.

"What do you mean?" Riley's eyebrows drew together as thoughts danced through her weary brain but refused to coalesce.

"Well..." he considered again, then set his own dishes aside and grabbed her foot in his hand, stripping off the sock and rubbing, gently working the knots and sore muscles. "I think maybe he's been infiltrating your mind since you were a child. Most kids don't stand still and let someone pound them. Not to mention, how did he always find you?"

Riley swallowed. "How did you know that? I used to try and try to hide from Danny, but no matter what, he was always there. Russell, I never told you that. How did you know?"

"I, uh..." his copper cheeks darkened. "I guessed. I used to do it to the other cubs. Enter their minds to find out where they were hiding when we were playing. I didn't hurt them, and they didn't seem to realize what I was doing. Later, my father taught me not to do that. To ask permission and accept refusal. I was just a kid playing games, though."

"I understand," Riley said, thinking over what he had told her. "Kids often do ill-mannered things, not realizing how rude they are. I suppose we'll have a few of those things to work through with our own daughter." She laid a hand on her belly, which had begun to curve noticeably outward. Then she groaned as Russ hit a particularly tender spot in her foot.

Once the tension had been drained away, he reached for the other. Riley let him. *It's nice to have a man who wants to spoil me sometimes.* "So you think Danny would... read my mind, so he could find me?"

"It seems likely. I know he's a dreamwalker. We've established that. Dreamwalkers usually have other extrasensory skills. Since I have both dreamwalking and telepathy, it stands to reason others could have the same combination of abilities. Listen, Riley." He set her foot off the side of the sofa and reached for her hand, pulling her upright to sit beside him. "Imagine a scenario. I don't know if it's true, but see if it resonates."

"Okay."

"Imagine your brother, a strong natural telepath and dreamwalker, but completely untrained. Clearly he also has some sort of personality disorder. I don't know which side of the family the ability comes from. If it's his unknown father, then you didn't inherit it." He thought again. "Wait, no. You have it too. You're a dreamwalker, though you try to suppress it. And we could communicate long before the cord between us became so strong. It must have come from your mother, who also had something a little off about her. Sometimes, gifts like these, if they're very powerful, can be damaging to the psyche. Unfettered psychic power..." he shook his head.

"You don't need to say more," Riley said tersely. "I get the idea. But if this particular version of psychic ability causes madness, why am I not crazy?"

"Because you have a different father," he replied. "A gentle soul, right? Not to mention, a spiritual leader. He would have been able to help you learn good values and self-control. He may well have been a psychic null, one with no ability whatsoever. That would have appealed to your mother. Those who are unbalanced seek balance."

"Okay, that makes sense," she replied. "But then, why did being with father not help mother balance? I don't have many memories of her, but I do recall her getting worse and worse."

"I don't know," Russ replied. "You're right, that shouldn't have happened. Not unless she sustained some kind of psychic damage. But this is all speculation."

"Yes," Riley agreed. "Though I have to admit, it's interesting in a bizarre way." She fell silent, pondering the information that might just explain so many of her problems. Then she gasped. "Oh God."

"What, honey?"

"Is that why I gave my brother my inheritance instead of going to the police? I mean, what if I had signed the paper, and then gone to the police the next day and pressed charges for assault and attempted robbery? Why did I not think of that option until now?"

"What do you mean?" Russell's snowy eyebrows drew together, crinkling deep furrows between his eyes and in his forehead.

"What if he projected so much terror and such a sense of threat into my mind that I couldn't think straight?"

Russell blinked. "You know, that does make sense. Riley, your brother is a very sick man."

"I know," she replied. "Why do you think I want to stay as far from him as possible?"

Russell sighed. "I wish we had met sooner, you and I. There are all kinds of ways for you to prevent him from entering your mind. Even expelling him if he finds his way in. Father told me he's found out some information about it."

"Tell me," she insisted. "He's looking for me, Russ. I need to know how to stop him from doing what he does. I can't have him rendering me docile and terrified. Who knows what he might take a notion to do next."

"I will," Russell promised. "Let's get a good night's sleep, and tomorrow I'm taking you to the village. Father can tell us what he's learned. Get rested up. It's a strain, doing psychic work, and I don't want you to wear yourself out."

There was sense in what he was saying, and Riley nodded slowly. "Okay, that's a good plan. I'm actually looking forward to it."

"Me too. I'm sure you'll find it empowering to be able to keep him away on your own. In fact, I can't believe we've taken this long to explore metaphysical solutions. I was treating you like a null, but under the circumstances, that was a foolish assumption. Father did say you have the power to control your own mind, to prevent attacks, but he didn't go into detail. I don't think he likes telephones." Russell shook his head. "I've been a dunce where you're concerned."

"It's okay," Riley insisted. "Who even thinks about things like this normally? We were so focused on Danny's dreamwalking… believe me, I didn't consider that I might have telepathic powers too."

"It explains a lot about why we're mated," he pointed out. "Our abilities seem pretty well matched in that area. Not to mention you're just a wonderful person."

Riley beamed. “You’re not bad yourself.” Then she giggled, suddenly bubbling with energy and enthusiasm. “I’ve heard girls describe their boyfriends as the teddy bear type, but nothing like this.”

Russell concealed his grin behind a scowl. “I’m no teddy bear.”

Riley rose to her knees and straddled Russell’s lap. “You’re cuddly like one. And you comfort me when I’m upset. I think you’d better just own the title, sweetie.”

His roaring, ursine laugh burst through. Riley captured it in a long, wet kiss.

He pulled back. “I thought you were tired.”

“Not anymore,” she replied.

He quirked one eyebrow. “Have energy to burn?”

“Do I ever. Isn’t that weird?”

“Riley, when it comes to your pregnancy, nothing strikes me as weird anymore.” His hands slid from where they’d landed on the small of her back, around to her belly and then upward, cupping one breast in each hand. “I’d better drain off some of that excess so you can sleep. We have a big day tomorrow.”

"I like that plan," she agreed. "Come on. Let's get ready for bed. I'll probably crash the moment we're done."

"You probably will," Russ agreed. He kissed her lips once, anticipation burning in his dark eyes. Riley slid off his lap and rose, grasping Russell's hand and leading him toward the bedroom with its attached en suite. *Better brush my teeth and wash my face quickly. Who knows how long this little lift will last?*

In fact, Riley's concern proved to be accurate. By the time she slid back the covers on her bed, she was beginning to droop. Russell joined her, taking her in his arms. She nestled her head against his shoulder. *I love how big and strong he is.* He claimed her lips and she melted in his heated embrace. Feeling boneless, Riley allowed Russell's strength and warmth to sink in to her, filling her with deep contentment.

"Are you too tired, honey?" he asked.

"No," she replied. "I want you… just… is slow and easy okay?"

He laughed his rumbling laugh. "Of course, Riley-girl. Do you think there's a way I don't want to love you?"

He tugged her sweater up over her head and unhooked her pants so she lay in her underwear, waiting. She watched unabashedly as he dragged his jeans down his slim hips and over his muscular thighs. Despite her fatigue, Riley's mouth watered at the sight of Russell's thick erection tenting the front of his boxers. Her insides clenched and wet heat surged between her thighs.

"You look so pretty, Riley-girl," Russell said, his voice a sexy growl. "When you lie there in your underwear and your eyes go all hot and dreamy." He took in a deep breath. "I can taste your arousal."

"I want you, Russ," she said, reaching out to him.

He went easily into her arms. She sighed.

"Is this what you want?" he asked, nuzzling her throat.

She tilted her head back on the pillow, granting him greater access. "It's the start of what I want."

He laughed again. "You sure have your way of making me feel like a man, Riley."

"You don't need my help," she replied dryly.

"No," he agreed. "But who doesn't like to hear they're making their loved one feel good?"

She smiled and then slid her hands down his bare back and pressed his bottom forward.

"Ready for more?" he asked.

Riley lifted her hips.

"Careful, honey. Don't squash the baby. I'll take good care of you. Just relax."

Russell braced his weight on one arm, and with the other opened the fastening of her bra, letting her pregnancy-swollen breasts spill free. She moaned at the release of pressure. Russell rubbed at the red marks on her skin, then leaned forward to kiss each one. His trailing lips eventually homed in on her nipples, which he licked with gentle laps of his tongue, tenderly stimulating each tender peak without causing the slightest sting.

He's so good at that, Riley thought. Her hands stroked up and down his back, feeling the bunched muscles under smooth skin, marveling that at a thought, he would be covered with thick, coarse fur. *Dream lover.* To have his love along with this great sex made it even better. Greater moisture gathered between her thighs.

She felt swollen with love and need, aching to join with her man.

"Riley…" he kissed his way down her belly, snagging her panties as he went, baring her to whatever sensual delights he felt inclined to visit on her eager flesh. Riley felt just as inclined to let him.

Tenderly he urged her thighs apart and crouched over her, leaning down to kiss the swell of her belly.

"I feel so big already," she said. "It's hard to imagine how much bigger I'm going to stretch."

"Hush, love. It's beautiful." He nuzzled her skin. His next kiss landed on the top of her mound. "Hmmm, you smell delicious, girl. I'm going to eat you all up."

"Eaten by a bear." She sighed. "I can think of worse fates."

Then her teasing turned to soft whimpers as he kissed her lips open and took his first taste of her. Her hips bucked against the intense stimulation, but he held her down with a hand on her hip and plundered her tender sex with long licks and teasing tickles of the tongue. He probed every fold from the wet entrance to her body all the way up to her clit and back down again. "You're so wet," he told her. "So wet and sexy." One thick finger slipped deep into her well, not to thrust in and out, but to rub a little spot of nerves so exquisite, her toes curled into the sheets. "You were made for this, Riley." He stopped talking then as his tongue claimed her clitoris with long, gentle licks. Each stroke drew a soft cry from her. Her orgasm built quickly, stoked by Russell's expert stimulation. His finger tickled her deep inside and his tongue mirrored the movement on her most sensitive spot.

"Come, baby," he urged. "Come hard. I want to taste it."

His sexy words drove her over the edge, headlong into ecstasy. Pleasure rippled from that secret spot deep within her, tightening her muscles and drawing cries from her mouth. Russell never let up for a moment. On and on he caressed her body until he had wrung every drop from her. Only then did he rise up, urging her to roll over into his favorite position. Though nearly totally drained, Riley lowered herself to her elbows and presented her sex for his taking.

"You, my love, are about to be mated by a bear," he told her solemnly, running proprietary fingers over her sex, and then spreading the folds.

"Yes, please," she urged. The sensation of Russell's thick sex inside her had become an addiction, and she wanted her fix of his love. Russ didn't disappoint.

Riley hissed through her teeth as her body yielded to his penetration. That first thrust still took her breath away every time. Biting her lip, she held still as Russ slowly pulled back, and when he surged forward again, she rocked back to meet him. The thickness of his sex spread her wide and he nudged deliciously on that special spot again. Riley squeaked at the pleasure. "Like that, little girl?" he asked her.

"Oh yeah," she moaned. They matched each other thrust for thrust. Riley loved this. Russ' big, warm hands on her hips, giving himself leverage as he rocked in and out of her. Riley braced on her elbows, desperate to have her man as deep inside her as she could. His love radiated like sunlight out of him and into her, merging their hearts, their souls, into a single being. Pleasure and emotion peaked at the same time, while Riley wept into the pillow and Russell marked her once more as his own.

By the time his orgasm and hers had waned, Riley could scarcely remain upright. Her wobbly knees threatened to give out on her. Russell's hand on her hip suddenly became a support as he withdrew his softening sex and eased her down onto the bed, on her side, and pulled the covers over them. With his warmth curled around her body, sleep took her before she even realized she was dozing.

Chapter 14

Russell couldn't help smiling down at his lady. She looked so sweet, asleep on the pillow, a shaft of moonlight illuminating her pretty face. That same moon called him, begged him to come outside and dance and pounce in its silvery light. The bear wanted to romp. *Only a short one,* he told the eager beast. *Tomorrow is a big day.* Rising, he kissed Riley on the forehead, slid his hand once over the small swell where their child grew within her, and eased from the bed.

Tucking the blankets up around Riley's chin, he moved silently through the house and out into the chill of the night. *Soon it will be getting too warm to want to go out in my fur, even at night.* He tolerated the heat because he loved to play, but he knew he needed to savor the coolness while it lasted. Outside, thick clouds crowded across the face of the moon and concealed the stars. Russell didn't need the light though. He found it easy enough to ramble along his familiar property and into the woods beyond. At last, the cold began to gnaw at his human skin, and he unleashed the bear. His body stretched and thickened, growing impossibly tall. He pointed his black nose at the sky and opened bone crushing jaws to let out an earsplitting roar. Rising to his full height, he sharpened his claws on the same poor, tattered tree before moving into an easy lope, his huge paws supporting his weight on the uncertain snow.

The clouds above swirled, sometimes parting to emit a hint of sky, sometimes concealing the heavens from his view, until a gap revealed the starry image of his goddess. Russell bowed his head before her visible form and uttered a prayer of thanks in the ancient language of the bears.

A whisper, a rare reply, seemed to echo in his mind. *Danger, danger. Return. What you love is threatened.*

Russell blinked, not sure what to make of such a message. *What danger?*

Hurry! the misty voice insisted. *Hurry… hurry!* The word repeated in endless litany in his mind.

He turned and ran for his house as fast as his powerful legs could carry him. In the clearing, everything seemed quiet. No sounds emerged from the house. *Was I panicking for nothing?* His nostrils flared. That same scent of garbage he'd noticed earlier seemed to have strengthened. *But it's inside a sealed can, where no creatures can get into it.* The stink thickened as a breeze blew past the door of the house. Russell nearly gagged. Loping toward his home, his heart began to hammer when he noticed the front door stood slightly ajar. He raced through, barreling past the kitchen and living room and into the bedroom, where he had left Riley, sound asleep.

The bed lay empty and crumpled, the comforter flung into the corner of the room, the sheets sagging to the floor.

Here, the garbage smell hung heavy in the air, seeming to belch like foul breath from the open door of the closet. Under its fetid stench, another, softer fragrance teased his nostrils. *Warm woman… recently bedded… Riley!* Russell stared, his mind refusing to draw any conclusions from the scene.

Following the trail of his lover's sweet aroma, he tracked, nose near the ground like a bloodhound, back through the house and out the still-open door.

Strange marks, rendered nearly unintelligible by many months of foot traffic, new snow, and more foot traffic, seemed to show a weighty figure in snow boots… and a strange parallel line between. The stink lay heavy on the ground. Desperate to make sense of the information, he followed the tracks to the shed. The lock had been cut. It lay, destroyed and forgotten, in a pile of pine needles. From there, the unmistakable impression of snowmobile skis cut a path into the trees and disappeared.

Already the scent, though visible, had clearly grown cold. At least half an hour had passed since they'd gone this way. *Bear or not, you'll never catch up with them if they've taken the sled.* His bear didn't care. Throwing his head back, Russell opened his huge jaws wide and shook the night with a roar of despair and rage. Then he rose to his feet and galloped toward town, just to one side of the snowmobile tracks. His heart pounded and his breath came in agonized gasps. His body, under the fur, grew too hot. But he never slowed his punishing pace, reaching town in record time. There, crisscrossing lines of traffic confused the images pressed into the snow, but the smell of his enemy still teased Russ, drawing him forward past the café, the church, the crumbling mansion where Riley had once lived, straight to the school's transportation yard. There, the school bus slept on the frozen asphalt. The tiny corrugated metal hanger also stood with its door ajar. The padlock had been cut, and bolt cutters lay in the snow beside his abandoned snowmobile. The scent was fresher here, as though not so much time had passed. Hopeful, Russ raced away from the transportation yard to the runway the school used. Sure enough, his plane sat on the tarmac, both doors open.

With an earsplitting bellow, he ran forward. On the far side, a large, unkempt man was struggling with a smaller, slighter figure, trying to stuff her into the passenger's seat. Both froze and looked up at him.

"Russell!" she screamed. The man stared for a moment in mute shock, then he delivered a powerful blow to Riley's jaw with one huge fist, stunning her. He shoved her into the plane, slammed the door and circled around to vault into the driver's seat. By now, Russell was only a few steps from the plane. He bounded forward, ready to pounce, but it seemed his enemy had studied airplane controls, because the little vehicle began to race down the runway. He couldn't keep up, though he tried. It bumped against the ground once, twice. The snowbank at the far end loomed. *Oh, God, no. Not a plane crash.* But the miscreant managed to manipulate the wing flaps and the plane roared into the sky.

Stunned, Russell sank back onto his haunches.

Unsettled thoughts raced aimlessly in a white swirl through his mind, not one coalescing into anything resembling coherence. *I have to do something. I have to… what?* He had to get help. That much was clear. *But you're a bear, Russ. Put clothes on.*

Despairing, furious and deeply afraid, he meandered back to the edge of town, circling around the edge within the tree line, until he reached his clothing stash.

Pulling inward on himself with his bear snarling death threats and fighting him with each passing moment, Russell forced the animal back inside the man. He quickly pulled on jeans and a sweater, shoes, jacket and hat before hiking into the police station.

Lips numb, he explained the situation to the dispatcher, a kind, plump woman sitting behind a desk. Though he knew almost everyone in Golden, her name escaped him, and he was so far gone, he never thought to consider her name tag.

"I'll get you an officer," she said. "Take a seat, please, Mr. Tadzea."

Russell sank onto the sofa in disbelief, his confusion slowly turning to rage. Rage at Riley's brother – because who else could have taken her? But also rage at himself for leaving her alone when she knew and had repeatedly told him Danny was trying to find her. *Idiot! How many times did you reassure her? How many times did you tell her to let her guard down, to trust you to watch her?* He had never imagined an outcome like this. *How the hell will they ever find her? There are hundreds of small planes in central Alaska. Dozens of official landing sites and who knows how many unofficial ones. Plus that idiot barely knows what he's doing. If they crash...* Nausea churned in Russell's stomach and tried to climb into his throat. He swallowed, not wanting to consider what could happen to Riley and their baby if Danny crashed the plane.

"Russ?"

Russell's head shot up. The uniform registered first. Dark blue button-up shirt with black tie, black slacks and a dark, bumpy hat. Then the trim figure and 40-something face came into focus and he stared into the dark, concerned eyes of Jack Morris, a man he'd been friends with for years.

"Jack, Riley's gone. You have to help me find her!"

* * *

Using every mental resource she had, Riley fought her way to full awareness. It was like swimming in a pool of cold molasses. She felt sluggish. Every thought tried to stick and cling. Through the haze she observed the familiar thick jaw, cleft chin and bull neck of her brother. His dark hair hung in greasy clumps and wild curls around his shoulders. A manic light shone in his blue eyes. He wore a ragged and tattered plaid shirt under an old, unzipped and heavily stained blue parka. The stench of him – sweat and stale cigarettes mixed with a goodly amount of booze – made her want to gag.

"Danny," she croaked, "what the hell are you doing? Turn this plane around and take me home."

The sticky feeling increased and a buzz sounded in her ears. She became dully aware that Danny was doing… whatever this was. His mind probed inside hers, controlling her. Muted rage churned in her belly, but she couldn't quite express it.

He laughed a rude and sneering chuckle. "Hell no, little sister. You have something I want, and you're not going home until you give it to me."

"I don't know what you're talking about," Riley groused. "I gave you everything. The house, the car, Dad's life insurance. Everything. There's nothing else and I told you that."

"You're a liar," he snapped. "You know exactly what I mean. A whore too. Imagine my surprise at finding my 'innocent' little sister, not sleeping alone in the shitty apartment listed on her forwarding address, but naked in some man's house, reeking of sex. When did you turn into a slut, Riley?"

Riley ground her teeth, the only expression of anger she could manage. "You're wrong," she replied, digging through her sluggish brain for an explanation. "Russell is my husband." *He is, at least in the way of bears. It works for me.*

"Bullshit," Danny snapped, and the plane jolted dangerously toward some trees. "You haven't been up there long enough to get married. And I never saw any invitation."

Riley snorted. "There's no such thing as 'not long enough.' Russ is special. I'm lucky to have him. And for your information, it was a small, private ceremony with no guests." She swallowed a bubble of hysterical laughter. *Small and private... as he mounted me from behind in front of the fire.* "You know, Danny, it was a really stupid thing you did, taking me out of my bed. Russ isn't going to let this go. You're going to regret it."

He laughed. "You can go right back home to your jackass 'husband.'" Danny made finger quotes in the air with one hand and the plane lurched. "As soon as you tell me what I need to know. If you'd just told me in your dream..." He turned to face her and the plane jerked sideways.

"Watch the sky, damn it," she snapped. "Do you even know how to use this thing?"

"Of course I do," he shot back. "I've been training on crop dusters for the last month."

"A month?" Riley shrieked. "You've been in training for a month, and now you're flying in unfamiliar airspace, in a remote, dangerous area, and you're not even paying attention. Have you ever actually flown on your own?"

"Cool it," Danny snarled. The fuzzy feeling in Riley's brain ramped up to a loud whine, like a thousand mosquitos trapped inside her head. Her temples began to throb. Over the noise, she could barely hear her brother say, "I've taken over the controls a couple of times."

"Have you ever landed?" Riley asked, groaning at the agonizing pressure.

"Once," he replied.

Oh Lord. Unable to speak, Riley stopped struggling and slumped against the window. *I can't distract Danny. I have to let him concentrate or he'll kill us both. Russell, please hurry and find us, baby.*

Chapter 15

Russell sat on his sofa, half-lost in pointless ruminations as the police puttered around his house collecting evidence. All the stomping of boots on his wood floors, which once would have driven him insane, now seemed utterly unimportant next to the task of retrieving his beloved. A touch on his shoulder brought him to startled alertness.

"Sorry," Jack said. "Can I sit? I have to ask you a few questions."

"I didn't hurt Riley," he gritted out between tightly clenched teeth. His jaws ached from the force, but he didn't relax.

"No one is suggesting you did. We all know how much you two love each other. It's been obvious from the beginning. But right now, we're trying to figure out what happened. You were the first to discover the crime. Help us reconstruct the events."

Russ nodded.

"Did you notice anything missing from the house… apart from Riley, that is?"

Russell did a mental inventory. "Actually, yes. Riley has a book. It belonged to her father. It was on the table here last night, but now it's gone. What is that idiot *doing*?!"

"I have no idea," Jack replied. "That's what you're going to help me with. When did you last see Riley?"

"I think it was about eleven."

Jack made a note. "Walk me through the evening."

Russ leaned his head back against the sofa and tried to pull himself together. "I picked her up at seven, after parent-teacher conferences. We came home, and Riley was exhausted. She slept on the sofa while I made dinner. Oh, um, and I took out the trash. It smelled bad in here." *You're rambling, Russ. Be careful what you say. They don't know you're a bear. If that gets out, you'll have worse troubles… like more angry bears tearing the house down, with you in it. You can't save*

Riley if you're fighting them. "Okay, well, so… we ate dinner on the sofa and talked and then we… um…" *Crap. I have to give away too much.* "We went to bed. We were… um… in bed for a while. Then Riley fell asleep." He broke off and looked up at his friend. Jack had one eyebrow quirked and his mouth was turned up on one side.

"Okay, then. What next?"

"I couldn't sleep. It was about eleven, I suppose. I wanted to get some fresh air, so I went outside. I don't know how long I was out. At least an hour. When I came back, the door was open and Riley was gone. The closet door was open, but I always keep it closed. Oh, shit."

"What?" Jack's head shot up.

"He… shit, shit, shit. He must have been in the closet all evening." Russell gulped. "He was right there when we were…" Nauseated and furious, Russ examined his fingernails, wishing he could unleash his claws and tear Riley's brother limb from limb.

"Calm down, Russ. How do you know he didn't come while you were out?"

Russell shook his head. "I was outside. It was so quiet… I would have heard someone approaching. The snow is so crunchy right now, you know? And if they'd brought a snowmobile or four wheeler..."

"Right. Noisy as hell. I see your point. So you think he was hiding in your closet? That's damned creepy, man."

"No kidding." Russ felt ill. To think he'd been laying his lady while her nasty brother hid a few feet from the bed. Jack seemed to have had the same realization because his mouth twisted into lines of disgust.

"Jack, you have to find her. She's pregnant, and alone with him. He used to beat her up."

Jack patted Russ on the shoulder. "I'm sorry. We'll get her back. So what did you do when you saw she was gone?"

"I noticed some tracks by the back door. Looked like boot prints and drag marks. I followed them to the shed, and my lock had been cut. My snowmobile was gone." He growled. "That asshole used my own sled to kidnap my girl."

"I know, Russ. I know. It sucks. Try to calm down. Then what did you do?"

"I tried to track them down. I followed the tracks all the way to town. I almost caught up. He had stolen the plane from the school district's transportation shed. He literally shoved Riley inside and took off as I was running toward them."

Russ shot Jack a pleading look.

Jack shook his head. "Sorry, man. Now, you know Riley better than anyone in town. You know about her brother, when no one else realized she even had one. What kind of person was he? You say he used to beat her? And where might he have taken her?"

Russ shook his head. "He's crazy. Beat the shit out of her as a kid. He went to prison a long time ago for a bar fight… involving a knife. Riley says she came here to get away from him. He threatened her with a knife and made her give him her inheritance from her father."

Jack's thick black eyebrows had drawn together. He stared.

"I know. Hell of a mess."

"Why would anyone beat up a girl as sweet as Riley?"

"Because he's freaking nuts," Russ replied, grinding his molars again.

"Sounds like it. Any idea what he might want?"

Russ sighed, choosing his words carefully. "She said he had been bothering her again, demanding she turn over 'what she stole from him.'"

"Wha..."

"I don't know," Russ cut off the question. "Riley figures he's flipped completely. He seems to think she managed to smuggle some part of the inheritance away from him, and he wants it."

"Was her father rich?"

Russ shook his head. "I don't think so. Riley said he was a scholar and a clergyman."

Jack shook his head. "I don't get it."

"Neither do I," Russ agreed. "I'm not sure even Riley did."

"But what you've told me does give us a place to start looking."

"Where?"

"Wherever her father lived. Do you know where that was?"

"Portland," Russ replied. "Portland, Oregon."

"Okay. Any idea on the brother's name?"

"Danny." Russ ran his fingers through his hair, making the white strands stand on end. "And more than that I have no idea. He's Riley's half-brother, so I doubt his last name is Jenkins. I'm not even sure if Danny is short for Daniel or something more unusual."

"It's okay," Jack replied. "We have Riley's previous addresses on her background check from the school district. If we can locate the father's house, it will give us a place to start."

"Would he take her somewhere so obvious?" Russell demanded. "That seems really foolish."

"So is creeping into a man's house and hiding in his closet, not to mention stealing his snowmobile, airplane and *girlfriend* right out from under his nose. He sounds like a narcissist and they're always overconfident. I think we have a good shot here."

Russell closed his eyes. He didn't know what to say next, but his composure was suffering. He could feel Riley's fear.

"Son." Russell's eyes shot open and his jaw dropped.

"Father?" Sure enough, the elderly Den'a man stood framed in his doorway. Norman stepped carefully into the room and made his slow way to the armchair, where he perched.

"How did you know to come?" Russ asked, stunned.

"A father knows when his son is in need."

Overwhelmed, Russ buried his face in his hands, elbows resting on his knees.

"Jack Peters, it is good that you are here. Help my son find his woman."

"I will," Jack replied. "Russ, I'm going to take off, back to the precinct and make some phone calls. Try to hang in there, buddy."

Russ didn't answer. He couldn't.

The sound of Jack shutting the door barely registered.

"Son." Russ looked up. His eyes felt like little balls of flame. "Call to your woman. You have the gift, do you not?"

"I do," Russ agreed. "That's why the bears threw me out, remember?"

"Yes," his father agreed. "I remember. I was glad you came. Being separated from a son is… hard on a father."

Russ wasn't sure what to make of the words, and focused as he was on Riley, he didn't want to take the time to think about it either.

Closing his eyes again, he took his father's advice. He entered the dream. Then he opened his mind to his beloved.

He found her easily, a ball of wild panic deeply suppressed under an oppressive aura of terror. The panic was her own, but the terror tasted of that garbage that had tainted his home.

"He's doing something to her to make her compliant," Russ said.

"Of course," came the reply, which now sounded distant and hollow, as though his father sat inside a metal tube. "He has a strong cord attached to her. He has used it to control her. It should have been cut long since."

"I suppose she doesn't know how," Russ replied. His consciousness probed at the aura until he found a weak spot and pushed through... and found himself sitting in his airplane, manning the controls while Riley cowered beside him. "Riley. Can you hear me, honey?"

She turned to regard him, eyes wild. "Russell?"

"Hang on. We're coming. Where are you?"

"Approaching Fairbanks," she replied. "At least I think so. I don't think he's planning to put down in the airport though. He keeps circling."

"Probably looking for a field, damn it. Riley, are you okay?"

"Yes," she whimpered. "He hasn't hurt me yet, but I'm scared. What if he hurts the baby?" Her hands went to her belly, cupping the small roundness there.

"Don't do anything to upset him. Try to figure out what he wants, or try to stall him. Whatever. Just don't make him mad. I'll get to you as quickly as I can. Any idea where he'll go next?"

"I don't know," she whimpered. "He keeps saying I know what he wants, that I know what I took from him, but, Russell, I didn't take anything."

"I know. I know. Just keep him busy until I can get to you. You can do this, Riley. Be brave. You know him. You know how to deal with him. I love you."

"Russell..."

Riley disappeared. The plane disappeared and Russell found himself in his living room again, staring at his father with unfocused eyes.

"He kicked me out."

"Is your woman safe?" the older man asked.

"I think so," Russ replied. "I hate this."

His father dipped his chin slowly. "Of course. But try not to panic, Russell. She needs you to stay calm. Did she say where they are?"

"She thought they were headed to Fairbanks," he explained. "Probably going to ditch the plane outside of town and try to get to the airport.

"Son, if she resists in such a public place, people might intervene," Norman pointed out.

"I don't know if she can." Russell made an unhappy face. "He has her locked down so tight, trapped in a dream, she's going to look like a zombie. Not to mention she's terrified he might take her resistance out on the baby."

"Do you really think they would go to Portland?" Norman asked.

Russell nodded.

"Then we should go there too. I will ask your brother to prepare the tribal plane. We probably will not arrive in time to prevent him boarding, but at least we should be able to follow closely."

"That's a great idea. Thank you so much, Father. Let me call Jack – God only knows how I'm going to explain this – and let him know we're going after her. He can call ahead to Portland."

Russell bounced up off the sofa, glad to have a plan of action at last.

* * *

Danny landed the little two-seat airplane in a field outside of Fairbanks with enough of a jolt to tempt Riley into giving up her breakfast, lunch and dinner. "You're a shitty pilot," she said, covering her terror with bravado.

Danny slapped her cheek, not hard enough to bruise, but enough to remind her to watch her mouth. "Get out."

"I'm in my pajamas," Riley whined. "I don't want to walk around like this."

"You're lucky," he replied. "Your pajamas look like some people's travel clothes." He waved at her sweatshirt and yoga pants. "And after all, I found you bare-ass naked."

"Yes, well," she replied, still sulking, "when you're asleep in your bed, you don't expect company. Not from your brother anyway. What's it to you if I sleep naked? Russell likes it."

"Riley, don't make me remind you again to be quiet," he snapped. "I don't want to hear about your whorish ways with that dirty old man of yours."

Riley considered arguing, but decided against it. If Danny lost what little control he had, they were both out of luck. "Can you tell me what it is you want, Danny?" Riley asked in her softest, gentlest voice. "Maybe if you explain what you're after, I can help you. Then I can go home."

"You already know, little liar. And you will tell me, later. Right now, Riley, you need to go to sleep."

Riley tried to resist, but somehow, her brother reached into her mind and dragged her into the dream. Standing on a flat, white plain with a featureless black sky and no scenery, he confronted her. "Don't try to get out. If you give me any trouble, I know where you're vulnerable. You have one chance to keep your kid alive, and that's to do everything I tell you. Understand?"

Riley nodded, though she was sobbing too hard to speak.

"You know, I think you had the right idea before. You kept me out for years with this. Now I'll keep that asshole ‘husband’ of yours out.” Danny waved his arms and the blank, fake-looking sky disappeared under a curving white dome. The igloo surrounded her once again, blocking her access to the rest of the macro-consciousness, but also blocking anyone else from reaching her there.

She was trapped.

Chapter 16

Despite being on the last leg of his flight to find Riley, Russell and his bear agreed that sitting in a too small airplane seat did not feel right. He wanted to roar, to slash things with his claws.

Warm, hard fingers rested on his arm. "Be at ease, son," his father said again. "Panic will not bring her back, nor remove her safely from her brother."

"I know," Russell growled. "It just kills me, Father. We've been in each other's minds and dreams since we met. Being shut out..."

"I know," Norman replied. "Your mother and I shared dreams for years. When she died..."

The old man fell silent. Despite his own distress, Russell couldn't help but notice his father's obvious grief. He had assumed his parents' mating had been more political than personal. *Looks like not.* He would never have been able to explain why, but the realization his parents actually cared for each other touched him.

"Is she well?" Norman asked, breaking into Russell's thoughts again.

"I have no way of knowing. I suppose the fact that she's shielded means she must be okay, right? If she was hurt or... or anything, he wouldn't need to do that." Russell swallowed hard and stared out the window at the clouds below them. Though the flight from Seattle to Portland was quite a short one, not being able to see anything but dense, fluffy darkness made him feel like he was drowning in cotton candy.

"It seems likely," his father replied.

"Use the cord," Randy, seated behind him, suggested.

Russ whipped his head around, which caused his neck to pop. "What do you mean?"

"You two have a cord as strong as steel between you. I can see it."

"I know," Russ replied. "It's always been like that."

"So use it," Randy insisted. "Dreamwalking is not your sole connection. I'd be very surprised if Riley's brother has even thought of it, and as much energy as he's expending keeping Riley trapped and shielding her inside a dream, he won't have anything left for that cord. Not that he would be able to anyway. Reach out to her along it."

Russell tried. Using the cord after so much experience in dreams felt uncomfortable, like squeezing into a pair of child-sized pantyhose, but he tried.

"Riley?" This way had no visual connection, though when he concentrated he could almost draw an image of her in his mind, curled into a ball, but seemingly floating in space. Her fear radiated from her.

"Russell?"

Startled by the echoing response in his head, he lost the connection. Opening his eyes, he made a face at his brother.

"Try again," Norman urged. "Don't give up."

Russell nodded and closed his eyes. "Riley, we're coming for you. We'll be there soon. Hang on."

"Russell, I'm scared." Her voice sounded so strange, hollow and distant. Russell rested his head against the window beside him and focused all his attention on the vicinity of his heart, the place where he connected to his woman.

"I know, honey. Are you hurt?"

"No, but he threatened me. Threatened to hurt the baby if I don't give him what he wants. Russ, I have no idea what he's after."

"I know you don't, honey."

"Russell." His father's voice broke into his mind, speaking to his consciousness directly. "She cannot just wait for us. She must have options to protect herself."

"Is that your father?" Riley asked.

"You can hear him?" Russell tried to reach out to her, but this method of communication didn't allow for contact. His fuzzy, non-corporeal hand slid right through her fuzzy, non-corporeal frame.

"I can hear him. It's like someone's voice in the background when you're on the phone. Can he hear me?"

"I can hear you, Riley," Norman said. "Listen, we are coming as quickly as we can, but there may come a moment when you can break free on your own. If you can, you must do it. This person is dangerous and unpredictable. You need to be away from him."

"I can't," she replied, her voice breaking. "He'll hurt me."

"He might try," Norman replied. "You're correct about that. That is why, Riley, if you have the chance to escape, you should take it. Obviously, if you're in a public place, anyone will help you. But I think he will control you until he has you in your father's home. Do you have a neighbor who will let you in, protect you from him? You may only get one chance, so you must get to safety quickly."

"Yes, anyone. All the neighbors know me," Riley said, and her panic had given way somewhat to consideration. Then fear resurfaced. "But it won't matter because he can enter my mind and make me do what he wants."

"I know." Norman's voice sounded grim. "That is why you must cut the cord between you. Look for it, but do not touch it. It probably enters your back."

"I can see it," Russell breathed. "It's black and ugly, like the tentacle of some kind of sea monster."

"It is evil," Norman commented. "It should have been cut years ago. He has been draining your energy all this time. He makes you exhausted by taking your strength. Then, when your soul goes into alert, he uses the cord and dreams to make you afraid."

"Yes," Riley agreed. "That sounds exactly right. So what do I do?"

"You wait. Stay alert for opportunities. I feel once you are in your home, he will lower his guard. He will let you return from the dream. He needs you to help him with what he is seeking. That is when your opportunity will arise. Until then, we will feed you energy through Russell's cord. He, his brother and I will pour life into you. You must hide it in your heart. Do not let your brother find it. It is yours and not for him. Save it up. It will help you feel stronger and more in control. Meanwhile, think of the baby, of caring for her and protecting her. That will give you strength. When your opportunity arises, send a huge pulse of energy all at once through the cord to your brother. This will startle him. Then dissolve his connection to you – imagine something hot cutting through it – and shield yourself."

"How do I do that?" she asked. "I don't know how to keep him out."

"It is a simple process," Norman told her. "It mostly requires concentration. Imagine a bubble around you. Anything he throws at you will bounce off. He will try to reconnect the cord, but if you concentrate on your bubble, he will not be able."

"That does sounds simple," Riley said doubtfully.

"The attack on your shield will be strong and you will have to fight hard to keep it," Norman warned. "That is why you must get away from him as quickly as possible. Get to a neighbor. Have them call the police."

"We should let the local police know to be looking for them," Russell said.

"They don't know already?" Riley demanded.

"We didn't know your address. The police are looking into your background check information to get your previous address. Can you tell it to us?"

Riley replied with a number and street name, and then added, "The car is almost at the house.

We'll be inside in a few minutes. Where are you all?"

"We're going to be flying into Portland in about ten minutes," Russell assured her. "We'll call the police from the gate and go directly to where you are."

"Okay," she said. "Russell…"

"I love you, Riley. I'm with you always. Hold on, honey."

"Get away if you can," Norman urged. "Do not stay long in his company. Think of the house, of its layout. Do not run for a door if a window is closer. Get outside quickly. The street is safer and someone else's house is safer yet."

"I understand," Riley replied. "I'll try. Hurry, please."

"We're coming as fast as we can," Russell insisted. "It won't be long now.

Russell sent a burst of energy along the golden cord that connected them. Riley's fuzzy internal image grew brighter. A small halo formed around her belly.

"Not too fast, son. You might choke her. A little trickle at a time."

"I know, Father," Russell replied. "I wanted her to get a jump start." He slowed the energy to a steady flow, strengthening her as best he could.

The plane began its descent into Portland International Airport.

* * *

The energy Russell was feeding into Riley made her feel better, stronger, and less like a zombie. While Danny still kept her consciousness trapped in a dream igloo, she knew now how to break free… or at least how to try. And she would try. For herself. For Russell. For their daughter. *I won't be mousy any more, baby girl,* she told the seed of life within her belly. *We'll get free.* Riley shivered. Facing down the brother who had always terrorized her made her feel ill. *But if anything happens to the baby because I'm too chicken, I'll never forgive myself.* The thought of her tiny, helpless daughter galvanized Riley's resolve. *When the time comes, I* will *protect her.*

* * *

"Little sister," Danny's threatening sing-song penetrated the walls of her icy mental prison. "Time to wake up now."

She shuddered and the image shattered, leaving her standing in her father's den. As in her dream, the room had been trashed. Tattered books lay on the floor. The door hung from only the lower hinges. Deep gouges marred the desk and the floor. Riley grieved to see the evidence of her brother's path of destruction through her father's beloved study.

"Okay," Danny drawled sarcastically, dragging Riley by means of a large hand clamped on her upper arm. "You say you don't know what I'm talking about? You say you aren't holding out on me? Then explain this!" He steered her toward a closet along the wall adjacent to the door and ripped it open. The accordion door slipped from its track and dangled limp beside them. Inside, below a row of tattered suit coats, sat a small plastic cube with a round dial of a combination lock set to one side of center.

"See," he said. "It's a safe. What was your old man hiding? People put valuables in safes. What's in there, Riley? Money? Jewelry? Guns?"

Riley shuddered at the thought of a gun in Danny's hands. "Did you know my father at all? He'd never have a gun. I don't think he had money or jewels either. Look at it, Danny. It's humidity controlled. If you took me from my bed in the middle of the night for a box of cigars..."

"Whatever. Just open it," Danny snapped, yanking Riley forward.

"How do you expect me to open it? I don't know the combination. I've never seen that safe before in my life." She dug in her heels and resisted his pulling.

"Liar," he snapped. "Your father told you everything. You practically lived in this room."

"Yeah," Riley sneered. "See that chair in the corner? I sat there reading a book. I didn't nose around in Dad's stuff. Besides, I was only here to get away from you."

Danny ground his teeth. "Open it."

"I'm telling you, Danny, you'd better take some of Dad's life insurance money and hire a locksmith. I don't know the combination."

The pressure in Riley's head increased until her ears were ringing.

"The noise won't help you, Danny," she shouted over the sound of a thousand bees, "I don't know the combination. If you torture me, threaten me, I still won't know the combination."

"And if I cut you up?"

Riley's head was vibrating so badly she struggled to see. The room seemed fuzzy, as though she'd gone out of focus. But she was able to understand that her brother had pulled something out of his pocket and was waving it her direction.

Knife, she realized, and her heart began to pound so hard, her chest hurt.

"Where should I start? Your little finger? Or do you want an emergency C-section?" He indicated her belly.

"Bastard," Riley hissed. "You wouldn't dare."

"Little sister," he murmured, his words almost getting lost in the hum that filled her brain, "do you honestly think there's *anything* I wouldn't dare to do? Now open it."

This is it, Riley. You won't get a second chance. Though she wanted to throw up from the tension, she drew in a deep breath. "You win, Danny. But you have to ease up the pressure. I can't see, let alone concentrate."

"Okay," he said, suddenly sounding jovial. A pleasant smile crossed his face. *Are you really that crazy, or are you just trying to freak me out?* The pressure in her head eased. Though she could still feel him, her life force draining into the ugly black cord she could now almost see stretching from her back to his belly, she could move a little more freely. And Russell siphoned a continuous flow of energy into her to compensate for what Danny was taking. She walked right up to the safe and fell to her knees. As she had hoped, Danny knelt behind her, watching over her shoulder as she reached for the dial. His hold on her mind decreased. His head was now directly behind hers.

Fast as she could, Riley threw her head backwards so the boney part of her skull smashed into Danny's nose. She drove her elbow, strengthened by one fist clutching the other, into his ribs. Bounding to her feet, she made a fast dash for the ruined office door.

The cord, damn it, or he'll own you for life. Imagining a burning sword in her hand, something like an angel would carry, she chopped at the black tube that connected them, severing the connection. Then she ran like hell down the hallway and toward the front of the house. *Got to get outside. Got to get to the neighbors'. Lord, please let them be home.*

The door seemed to appear out of nowhere, looming up in her face so she nearly crashed into it. Her breath wheezed in her heaving chest as she fumbled with the lock. Then an agonizing pressure on her scalp pulled her back.

"No!" she screamed, clawing at the fingers tangled in her hair. "No, Danny, stop!" She twisted her shoulders from side to side.

She could feel his sick consciousness slithering and oozing like an eel around the edges of her mind and realized she hadn't shielded herself. It was easy for him to plug in again. A pressure like nothing she'd experienced before threatened to rupture her eardrums. It felt as though she'd dived too deep under water. Riley grabbed her ears and screamed. The pain increased. Her eyeballs and temples throbbed. *He's going to kill me. He's going to blow up my brain.*

Deep within her, life stirred, a flutter like a butterfly tickling her from the inside with minuscule digits. *I have to live. I have to protect my baby.*

Without reflection, Riley let her consciousness slide along the cord into Danny's mind. As much time as she'd spent thinking in tandem with Russell, nothing could have prepared her for the mess she found in her brother. There were no smooth connections, no coherent flow of thought. Energy swelled and pooled like sewage around leaky pipes. His mind was a dark morass of decaying consciousness and rags of disjointed thoughts. Riley gagged. *With all this junk in his head, it's no wonder Danny's more than half crazy.* Distantly she became aware that her body was failing. Time was running out. It was Danny or her daughter, and she knew, without knowing how, what to do. The angel sword reappeared in her mental hand and she slashed and cut, breaking connections and severing off pieces of his mind from each other.

Now it was Danny who screamed. Riley didn't stop. She chopped away at his mind, reducing it to ribbons, until Danny's hands fell limp from her hair. She withdrew and returned to full awareness, using the sword one last time to cut the cord between them and bind off her end. Then she wrapped herself in a bubble of protection. Once again she turned to the door, only to run straight into a solid mass, one that seemed to reach out and engulf her. Still shaken, her limbs weak and rubbery, she still fought to free herself.

"Riley," a soothing and familiar voice rumbled in hear ear. The clean, inviting scent of safety washed over her. In the aftermath of terror, she began trembling violently, melting into a boneless mass in Russell's arms.

"I've got you, sweet girl. I've got you," he murmured as he slowly rocked her back and forth. Riley could feel people moving around her, and a dull roar of conversation rose and fell without her registering any of it. All she could feel, all she could focus on, was Russell's arms around her, holding her close.

One of the bodies drew near and she tried to flinch, but couldn't.

"What happened?" Russell's voice asked.

"Her brother… he has been taken to the hospital," another voice answered. Riley thought it might be Russell's father, but she couldn't tell for sure.

"To… why?"

"When we arrived, he was standing just down the hallway around the corner. Just standing there staring. Russell, she broke his mind."

Russell's hand circled on Riley's back. "She must have had a reason."

"I would say so. He had a knife in his hand."

"You wouldn't hold this against her, would you?"

Norman – she was now certain Russell's father stood beside them – laughed, a dry and humorless chuckle. "Anyone who threatens the cub will be killed by the mother. Riley is not a violent woman, and yet he was covered in blood, his nose broken and his mind destroyed. If he incited so much rage from her, he certainly deserved what he received. But I hope in time she will let us help her get past it. This will not be easy for her."

"She risked her life and attacked a violent, dangerous man to protect our baby," Russell pointed out. A warm touch on the top of her head seemed to be a kiss.

"I know, son. We will talk more later. For now, hold her and soothe her. She needs you."

"Okay, Father," Russell replied. "Come on, Riley. You need to sit down. You're shaking like a leaf." He released his hold so he could walk her to the adjoining living room, but her legs gave way and darkness closed in on her. As she collapsed, she thought she heard Russell say, "Oh hell." Then she passed out.

Chapter 17

Daylight filtered past Riley's closed eyelids, teasing her awake. She squeezed her eyes tighter shut and turned to her side with a protesting groan.

"Welcome back, Sleeping Beauty," Russell's voice murmured into her ear.

Riley's eyes snapped open, and she groaned again as the light stung her eyes. "Where am I?"

"I'm pretty sure this is the bedroom you grew up in," Russell replied. "I looked into the rooms here and I figured you wouldn't be comfortable sleeping in what must have been your father's, so I brought you here. The cowboy posters were a dead giveaway."

"Oh God," Riley moaned. "I decorated this room when I was fourteen and never changed it, okay?"

"Defensive much?" Russ teased. "I kinda like sleeping with all these half-naked men staring at me – not! No wonder you were so eager to have sex, silly girl."

"Shut up," she grumbled, burying her face in the pillow. "You weren't complaining."

"Nope," Russ agreed, kissing the back of her neck. "No man would complain about the privilege of tutoring a beautiful, loving woman about sex." His hand cupped her breast and his morning erection dug into her bottom.

All of a sudden, the inappropriateness of the situation struck Riley. "Wait, what's happening? Why are we peacefully sleeping in this bed? Where the hell is Danny?"

"Gone for good," Russ replied. "He's been taken into custody, though I don't think he'll ever come to trial."

"What?" Riley couldn't follow what Russ was saying at all.

"Riley, how much do you remember about yesterday?" he asked.

She closed her eyes. "Do I have to?"

"Yes. Don't block out reality, honey," he urged.

Sighing, Riley thought back. "Danny brought me here. There's a humidity controlled safe in my father's den. He thought I knew the combination, even though I've never seen the thing before. Instead of messing with it, I fought him. Cut the cord and tried to run, but he caught me. I think he tried to kill me using his mind. I don't know how else to describe it." She swallowed hard against the nausea.

"What did you do?" Russ asked, stroking her arm with his fingertips.

"I followed the cord into his mind and… well, I don't exactly know. I imagined myself cutting him up with a sword. Did it work? Or did you guys arrive in the nick of time? I don't remember anything else."

"Yes," Russ admitted. "It worked. You destroyed what was left of his sanity, Riley. He can never hurt you again. His best hope is to live out the rest of his existence in a hospital for the criminally insane. Father got a quick look and is pretty sure he'll never be able to take care of himself again, let alone bother anyone else. And don't tell anyone, but I think he may have severed whatever it is in Danny's mind that allows dreamwalking, just to be on the safe side. It's illegal, but under the circumstances, I don't think anyone would blame Father."

"I might as well have killed him," Riley said softly, appalled at the horrific aftermath of her ordeal.

"It's true," Russell said. "But like killing someone in self-defense, what you did was justified. No one is angry at you, Riley. You were so brave. You protected yourself and our baby from him."

His hand had stopped groping her breast long since. Now he moved down to cup her belly. Again that small sensation fluttered inside her. Russ drew in a sharp breath. "Oh wow. Riley, honey... will you marry me?"

Riley blinked. "I thought we already were married." Then she thought for a moment. "Oh yeah, we are and we aren't, right?"

"Right," Russell agreed absently, still feeling the movement of their daughter under his hand.

"Russell... do you think your father would do it?"

"Do what? Marry us?"

"Yes."

Russell kissed her temple. "Riley, I love you," he said, and let her feel with him the joy her suggestion had caused.

She turned to face him, looked into his beloved face. "I love you, Russell. I love you so much."

She drew his lips down to hers. Then she broke away, embarrassed. "I need to brush my teeth."

"Okay," Russell agreed easily. "Do you think there are toothbrushes in here somewhere?"

"Yes," Riley nodded. "I always had extras on hand in case a friend slept over. I doubt Danny would have been interested."

Russ made a face. "He had a stink that wouldn't end. I'm sure you're right. Let's get cleaned up and dressed. Then we can figure out what to do next."

"Okay," Riley agreed. Rising uncomfortably from the bed, she groaned. Every joint and muscle ached. She staggered down the hall into the bathroom where, sure enough, six toothbrushes waited in their packages. She ripped one open, added toothpaste from a tube that was probably expired, but still sealed, and shoved it into her mouth with a relieved sigh. Then she caught sight of herself in the mirror. Her hair stuck out in all directions, she had pillow marks on her face, and her pajamas were dirty and crumpled. *I have nothing with me but what I'm wearing. I wonder if I have any clothes left in the closet. I wonder if they'll fit over you, little girl.* She stroked her belly while she brushed her teeth.

Russell joined her and she indicated the medicine cabinet. As he brushed, she spat and returned to the bedroom, opening the closet and finding only one possibility – a flowered sundress with a stretchy top and loose skirt. It barely fit, and of course, she could find neither underwear nor bra to accommodate her changing shape. Shrugging, she pulled a button-up sweater onto her arms and stepped into bedroom slippers.

Russell returned to the room. "Riley, honey, do you know an attorney?"

"Yes. My father's best friend is one. He wrote Dad's will. Why?"

"I think you need to contact him. Let him know what happened with Danny and try to get whatever it is you signed declared invalid so you can have your inheritance back. You could… you could come back here. Live in your family home."

Riley thought about it and then shook her head. "I couldn't. I have good memories here, but a lot of bad ones too. Especially now. Besides, Golden is my home. I love it there. I would neither leave you nor ask you to live so far from your family. I'd prefer to sell the place. Maybe another family can replace the bad energy with something more positive."

"So you're definitely coming home then?" he asked, sounding a bit vulnerable. She moved into his arms and pulled him down to complete the kiss they'd begun earlier.

"Definitely," she replied.

For a long moment, the couple refrained from speaking, intent on reconnecting after their unplanned separation.

The tight embrace eventually loosened to make room for hands to wander over and then under clothing. Russell tugged Riley's sweater off her shoulders and dropped it to the floor. Next the thick straps of her sundress surrendered to his fingers and he tugged the top down, baring her breasts.

"Come on," Riley urged, pulling him to the bed. He shucked his clothing before joining her.

She grabbed his hands and placed them on her breasts. "Touch me," she urged.

Russell claimed her lips again, gently molding the swollen globes in his hands, and then shifting so he could thumb her nipples.

Riley sighed at the sweet stimulation as moisture surged between her thighs. *I want him in me so bad.* She arched her hips against him, her hands moving to his buttocks to press him closer.

Russell groaned. "Easy, Riley."

"I want you," she begged, releasing his bottom so she could grasp his penis, stroking it hard and fast.

"Whoa, girl." He grabbed her hands and pinned them over her head in one of his, rolling her onto her back and straddling her knees.

"Russell..." she whimpered.

"Hush, love. I was so worried for you. I'm going to feast on every inch of you, starting with these pretty breasts."

He lowered his head and caught one nipple between his teeth, lashing it with his tongue.

Riley sighed with pleasure, then sighed again as he moved to the other side. She squirmed, but he held her fast, insisting she accept his caresses, preventing her from returning the favor.

Then, in a sudden movement, he released her and hiked her skirt to the waist, pulling her thighs wide apart.

"Oooh," she moaned, knowing what was coming. Sure enough, Russell's fingers slid through her wetness, spreading it and then delving deep into her well. Riley's moan turned into a shriek as his mouth closed around her clit.

"That's it, honey. Scream for me. I'm going to make you come so hard." He eased a second finger inside her and set to work.

Riley's toes curled in the sheets as her man went down on her with exquisite skill. He lapped and teased the tender nub as he tickled her g-spot.

Tension coiled in Riley, hastening her toward the promised peak. She wept and whimpered but made no attempt to fight the pleasure. Russell showered his love onto her, not only with his powerful lovemaking, but with his mind as well, shedding golden light on the fragmented parts of her psyche. Pleasure and love swelled and surged in her, tightening her down and down until coiled ecstasy sprang free and she was whole, healed and happy; darkness banished from her soul.

Only then did Russell withdraw his fingers, strip her dress off completely, and roll Riley onto her hands and knees. She lowered herself to her elbows, presenting her still-clenching sex to her bear, eager to be mated by him. Russell's big hands captured her hips. He thrust hard, stretching her open with his thick erection. Riley squealed into the blankets. His rhythmic surges reignited her waning orgasm, leaving her weeping in ecstasy, her face buried in sheets that smelled of her man. Of herself. Of their love. In and out he moved with forceful grace, pleasuring her body and feeding her soul all at once, until with a window-rattling roar, he ejaculated, pouring his life essence into her body.

Then he gently lowered her to the bed and curled against her back. "I love you, Riley," he rumbled, his hand splayed on the outward curve of her belly.

"Hmmmm," she hummed in utter relaxation, the aches of her ordeal fading. Many long minutes passed before she spoke again. "Russell?"

"Yes, honey?"

"I need a shower."

"So do I," he said. "But you go first."

"No, you go," she said. "I want to lie here a while longer."

He chuckled, kissed her cheek, and hoisted himself from the bed.

* * *

Russell looked up from the book he was reading, seated on a comfortable sofa he'd found in the living room of the bungalow. Despite the havoc Danny had wrecked on the once-cozy home, a few places remained livable. Russ' stomach growled. *Have to get something to eat soon. There's nothing worth mentioning in the kitchen, and I bet poor Riley is starving.* But first, he had something quick and important he wanted to share with her. He met her eyes and in a heartbeat he was hard once more, ready to bend her over the sofa and claim her again and again. The knowledge that she was naked under the clingy sundress tortured him. *Down boy,* he told himself fiercely. *You have a lifetime to lay your lady.*

Give her a minute's peace. We have more important things to do right now.

"Riley, you said your brother was after the combination to the locked safe in your father's study, right?"

"Yes," she replied, twisting a strand of wet hair around her finger. "But I have no idea what it is. I didn't even know Father had a safe."

"Did you know Danny took your father's book?"

She shook her head. "He blotted out the protective herbs around the house and under the bed, and stole my pillow. I was too tired to notice, remember? So by the time he took me, he had me so deep in dreams, I had no idea what was going on. I woke up on your airplane. Why would he take that? It's just a dusty old book."

"Because despite being crazy, Danny wasn't an idiot. It's a dusty old book, yes. One riddled with margin notes. I bet he was hoping, if you wouldn't or couldn't help him, to find the combination in these pages. Did you notice how he'd torn every book in the den off the shelves?"

"I did, now that you mention it," Riley replied.

"Was your father the sort who remembered things easily, or did he tend to write everything down?"

"Oh, he made notes for everything," Riley replied. "He always said 'a mental note isn't worth the paper it's written on.'" She gave a wistful chuckle at the memory. "He made notes about where he had placed his notes. Why?"

"Then it stands to reason he would have jotted down the combination to his safe's lock, right?"

"Oh yes," Riley agreed, then her eyes widened. "Do you think it's in this book?"

He nodded. "Makes sense. This was his favorite, right? I bet he always had it at hand."

"Oh, he did," Riley agreed, drawing closer. "Always."

"And sure enough, on page 252, I found a curious set of three numbers." He extended the book.

She regarded the top right hand margin and her eyes lit up. "Do you think those are it?"

"Shall we find out?" Russell countered.

"Oh yes!" Riley clapped her hands together.

Russ levered himself up off the sofa and took Riley's hand. Together they moved into the den.

Russell knelt before the safe and reached out. "Do you want to do the honors?" he asked Riley.

She shook her head. "I almost died for whatever is in this safe. I don't think I'd be able to touch it."

"Fair enough." He twirled the lock past zero and landed on thirty-seven. Then he turned it to the right and stopped on five. Last, he went directly to twenty-three, and pulled on the handle. The door swung open. Russell stared in shock. Riley, who had perched on her haunches to watch, sat down hard on her bottom, laughing until tears streamed down her face.

Inside the safe sat two old and tattered books with faded gold leaf embossing. One appeared to be a Bible, of the old-fashioned type that had family records inside the cover. The other was a copy of *The Pilgrim's Progress*, signed by Billy Graham. While both were certainly personal treasures, neither had any particular monetary value. Russell doubted the set would have brought $200.00.

"This was what he was after?" he asked, stunned.

Riley couldn't speak, but she nodded vigorously.

"I take it back. Your brother was an idiot after all."

A deep rumble began to shake Russell's chest. It burbled into his throat and spilled out of his mouth in a roar of ursine laughter. Clutching Riley to him, the couple laughed and laughed until laughter blended with tears.

Epilogue

Summer had finally melted the snow blanketing the Athabascan village. Prairie flowers bloomed in wild profusion between the houses and into the unclaimed land, stretching as far as the eye could see in all directions. In such a setting of perfect, natural beauty, any further adornment would have appeared tawdry, or so Riley thought as she stood before the creek. Behind her, natives and werebears in human form gathered in a horseshoe configuration. On Riley's left, Nasnanna, who had quickly become one of her closest friends, stood arrayed in a white fringed and embroidered dress over matching leggings, her baby perched on her hip. To her right, Russell beamed at her, gorgeous in khaki pants that clung to his muscular thighs, a white shirt and a fringed doeskin jacket, also heavily embroidered and beaded. His brother, similarly attired, waited behind him. A cool breeze, fragrant with pine and flowers, snaked its way down a distant mountain to ruffle the hair and dresses of the guests. Riley pulled her shoulder wrap a little tighter around her. Beneath it, the lacy straps of her loosely cut white tea length dress offered no protection from the chill. Despite the cold, she couldn't stop smiling as she slipped a simple band of rugged Yukon gold onto Russell's left fourth finger. His father spoke, intoning words Riley would never remember. All she knew at this moment was the love in his eyes. The certainty in his voice as he spoke his vows, vows that meant nothing, as the commitment had long since been established. She knew the warmth of his hand, which mirrored the warmth of the sun on her head, defying the chilly breeze. She knew the weight of their child nestled in her belly, a squirming heaviness that filled her with endless wonder. She had learned peace, safety and love for the first time in her life because of this man.

Russell leaned in over her expanding girth and kissed her lips, sealing their vows. Cheers and roars erupted all around them.

Riley had never doubted her decision to sell her childhood home, and this moment confirmed what she'd always known. The buyers, a couple who had adopted their two granddaughters, had been delighted to get a cozy family home at a good price. And Riley, after setting up a fund to provide her brother with a spot in a group home, had been happy to put the rest into savings for her baby's future. The little girl, who they'd decided to name Skye Angelica, would be able to pick from any university in the country, as would any siblings they might provide her in the future. *More babies… I hope Russ wants a few.* Riley could picture them now, snuggled up on the wooden-armed sofa under a blanket, eating popcorn and screaming at silly horror flicks. She sniffled as Russell turned her to face his family, and her hand flew to her throat, touching the loose choker of dentalium shells and below it, the thin chain that supported her black jasper amulet. Upon their return from Portland, Russell had found it flung in a corner, which explained at last how Danny had managed to get so deep into Riley's mind.

Shaking off the unwelcome thought, she smiled for their wedding guests. So much had changed since her arrival in Alaska, all for the better. Now, at the beginning of a new journey, Riley finally had found a home.

Dear Reader,

I hope you have enjoyed your romp in the Alaskan wilderness with Riley and Russell. What a fun couple. When they appeared out of nowhere demanding to be written, what could I do besides agree? And I'm so glad I did.

If you enjoyed their journey as much as I did, I'd appreciate it greatly if you'd let other people know, and head over to Amazon.com to leave a review. There is no greater gift a reader can give an author than honest feedback.

As far as the background of this story, I did a great deal of research on the Athabascan people in order to make Russell's family seem life-like. Of course, his particular group lives in secrecy and isolation because of their close alliance with the werebears, so any differences between them and better-known groups is certainly due to that.

The information about psychic phenomena, telepathy, cords and dreamwalking come from a dear friend who literally wrote the book on the subject. For information in the non-fiction form, be sure to check out Empath Basics by Sandra Martinez. It's a fascinating read, and certainly manageable enough even for a novice like me.

Thank you again for the time you put into reading my book.

Love always,

Simone

Dear reader,

We hope you enjoyed reading *Polar Heat*. Please take a moment to leave a review, even if it's a short one. Your opinion is important to us.

Discover more books by Simone Beaudelaire at
https://www.nextchapter.pub/authors/simone-beaudelaire-romance-author

Want to know when one of our books is free or discounted? Join the newsletter at
http://eepurl.com/bqqB3H

Best regards,

Simone Beaudelaire and the Next Chapter Team

Polar Heat

ISBN: 978-4-86747-353-5 (Large Print)

Published by
Next Chapter
1-60-20 Minami-Otsuka
170-0005 Toshima-Ku, Tokyo
+818035793528
27th May 2021

Lightning Source UK Ltd.
Milton Keynes UK
UKHW041913150621
385583UK00001B/54